MIDNIGHT BLUE

Midnight Blue is a haunting and beautiful story, full of mystery yet firmly rooted in the world we know. It is the story of Bonnie, whose fragile happiness with her mother Maybelle is shattered by the arrival of Grandbag. It is a story of escape. . .

With the help of Michael and the Shadowboy, Bonnie finds the world she had dreamed of, the world beyond the sky. A real family and a new friend – Arabella – await her: strange reflections of the world that Bonnie has left. But the cruelty of Grandbag follows, threatening Bonnie's new-found happiness.

Help comes from the mysterious Shadowboy, and from Edric and Godda, the ancient, elusive lord and lady of the hill. But Bonnie alone must meet the challenge and face the choices. . .

PAULINE FISK lives with her architect husband and five children in an old, red-brick Shropshire cottage, in an English village between the hills she writes about. She has written short stories and radio plays, as well as articles for magazines. She enjoys solitary occupations – riding her bicycle, walking her dog, making large tapestries on her weaving loom, and reading – as well as all the fights and fun and chaos of everyday family life.

MIDNIGHT
BLUE

Pauline Fisk

A LION PAPERBACK
Oxford · Batavia · Sydney

Copyright © 1990 Lion Publishing

Published by
Lion Publishing plc
Sandy Lane West, Oxford, England
ISBN 0 7459 1848 4 (Casebound)
ISBN 0 7459 1925 1 (Paperback)
Lion Publishing Corporation
1705 Hubbard Avenue, Batavia, Illinois 60510, USA
ISBN 0 7459 1848 4 (Casebound)
ISBN 0 7459 1925 1 (Paperback)
Albatross Books Pty Ltd
PO Box 320, Sutherland, NSW 2232, Australia
ISBN 0 7324 0198 4 (Casebound)
ISBN 0 7324 0269 7 (Paperback)

First edition 1990
Paperback edition 1991

Printed in Great Britain
by Cox and Wyman Ltd, Reading

Contents

PART ONE

Running Away

1

It began as it always did with sweet, solitary notes of music that called to her from somewhere beyond the sky, a single piper's cry that reached down for her and scooped her over roof tops and streets, office blocks and electric pylons, railway stations, shops and parks. The world faded beneath her. It was a hot, clear day and she flew up till she could see none of it any more. As she rose the sun rose with her, as if they were racing for the top of the sky. Its warmth welcomed her, caressed her skin. Above her the music of the lonely pipe, the only sound left in the whole world, drew her on until she prepared to hit the very roof top of the sky itself. Then the smooth sky puckered into cloth-of-blue and drew aside for her, like curtains parting. The music called again and she passed straight through.

Straight through, that is, into her bedroom. Bonnie came to herself and she was sitting on the floor, surrounded by a litter of suitcases out of which her childhood possessions spilled. A raggedy doll lay in her hands. She stared at it, momentarily bewildered, and then she knew that this was her new home, that she had unpacking to do, that it was a hot, still day beyond the open window, that she'd lost herself daydreaming again.

She shook her head. The pipe music faded away. She could hear instead the sound of Maybelle singing in the room next door, of furniture being dragged about, of the radio chattering in the kitchen. She got to her feet, put the doll upon the shelf, leaned out of the window. She could hear sparrows chattering, children playing, the droning of a vacuum cleaner next door now, traffic on the road outside the block of flats. She looked down beyond the balcony, at the tarmac forecourt and the sign that said HIGHHOLLY HOUSE Nos. 1-79. She followed the line of the orange brick wall along the road and behind the garages, past the cluster of trees in the corner, to the new shops.

There was something about those trees. Her eyes returned to them. What was it? They were stiff, gnarled, spreading hollies. Perhaps it was their obvious, stooping age that set them apart. Their branches trembled nervously in what seemed to be their own, private breeze. They were lonely, like a distant island across the sea . . .

Bonnie's mother opened the bedroom door. Her hair was piled into a straggly yellow whirl on top of her head. Her cheeks were round and pink. Her eyes were smudged with yesterday's mascara.

'Come on Bonnie, you wretch,' she said. 'Don't just sit there. There's lots to do.'

'All right Maybelle.' Bonnie turned from the window. 'I was just starting.'

'Well, hurry up with it,' her mother said. 'And think about colour schemes while you're at it. We'll go and buy some paint this afternoon.' She rubbed her hands against her jeans and tilted her head thoughtfully to look the room up and down. Bonnie looked at it too.

'What d'you think of red and yellow, Maybelle?'

Maybelle opened her mouth to tell her, but something stopped her. A car rattled across the forecourt. It halted right beneath the bedroom balcony and the happy colour faded out of her cheeks. Bonnie looked out of the window. She'd recognized the sound as well. She knew what she'd see.

'It's Grandbag.'

9

'On her own?'

'No. Doreen's with her.'

'Oh.'

They looked at each other miserably.

'She's probably missing you,' Maybelle said.

'I've only been gone one day,' Bonnie replied.

'I'd better go and put my make-up straight,' Maybelle said. 'She always says I look like I'm not coping when I don't.'

She left the room. Bonnie heard her humping the vacuum cleaner into the hall cupboard. She turned the kitchen radio off and there was an awful silence. Bonnie looked down again. Grandbag was hoisting straight her black-and-bead coat, which she wore whatever the weather, and readjusting her hat. Doreen, thin, dark and as different from Maybelle as a sister could be, fluttered round her in a shapeless bundle of a summer dress. Grandbag strode towards the stairway. Doreen followed her. Like an army of two, they disappeared into the darkness below. Bonnie heard Maybelle in the bathroom now. There was a waiting hush, then the shrill ring of the bell.

'We can't stay long. We thought we'd better come and see how you're managing with the child. You can show us round as well. How's she getting on?'

Bonnie heard them coming down the hall. 'She talks to herself,' she heard Grandbag say. 'You'll have to do something about that. And she daydreams.'

Almost without thinking, she climbed out of the window onto the balcony. They entered the room. She crouched out of sight. Close to the window, she heard Grandbag's voice again.

'What a mess! She won't do a thing if you don't make her, you mark my words. Where is she?'

She could imagine Grandbag hauling her coat straight again, and folding her emphatic arms in that gesture of hers. She could imagine the make-up, thickly caked to hide her creeping age. She could imagine the thin lips, the wobbling hat, the eyes . . . She flattened herself against the wall and heard her mother say that she'd been here a minute ago, that she didn't know where she had gone.

'You should have left the child with me,' Grandbag said. 'It's not going to work, you mark my words. Now you can't even find her. Do you know what she said to me, before you came to get her? Do you? She said, "Is Maybelle really my mother?" That's what she said. You should have left her with me, where she belongs.'

Bonnie could imagine Maybelle's face, bright with hurt feelings. She hung her head with shame and tried to slide away. Grandbag wasn't lying. She *had* said it. But she'd only wanted to be sure. She hadn't meant any harm. She found the fire escape at the end of the balcony, and jumped onto it.

'The trouble with you . . . ' Grandbag was saying, but Bonnie's shoe hit the metal step, and it rang out sharply, and Grandbag stopped.

'What was that?'

'I don't know.'

Grandbag and Doreen stuck their heads out of the window. Bonnie began to clamber down as fast as jumbled hands and legs would go. Grandbag's whole head shook with indignation, but she didn't call to Bonnie. She didn't ever speak to her, if she could help it. She shouted at Doreen instead.

'Get her, Doreen. Bring her back up here.'

Doreen clambered dutifully onto the balcony and began to wave her arms at Bonnie.

'Come back,' she called, in her thin, uncertain voice. 'Come back to your Grandmother right away . . . ' Bonnie, for answer, jumped the last few steps onto the ground.

'Maybelle, what does the child think she's doing?' Grandbag shouted. 'You've only had her a day, and she's running riot.'

11

Bonnie didn't hear any more. New sounds rushed to greet her, little kids skipping and roller skating and kicking cans, a gang of girls laughing together behind their hands, boys riding up and down on bikes in front of them. Doreen began to clatter down the fire escape and, without really thinking, Bonnie ran between the children and towards the corner and the holly trees.

The boys stopped kicking cans. The girls stopped laughing. Bonnie saw that the skaters had stopped skating, that all the children's heads were turned to watch her. Doreen was on the ground now, and shouting at her.

She reached the trees, and with some relief slid into their shade. They were dense and prickly and she struggled through. It was immediately quiet, as if she were a million miles away from children playing and the traffic on the road, as if she'd entered, not a cluster of rambling city trees, but a forest.

She came to a wall. There was so much ivy growing on it that at first she didn't realize what it was, and almost stumbled into it. It was an old wall, not searing orange brick like the wall up the road, but grey, ancient, flinty stones that rose up over her head. She could see trees swaying on the other side of it, and she began to make her way along, looking without success for a gate. Doreen panted behind her and, in her panic, Bonnie tripped over a pile of stones at her feet. She was about to climb over them, when she realized what they signified.

'There's only one reason why they'd be there,' she thought. 'They've fallen out of the wall!'

She began to dig into the ivy. Her arm plunged in, right up to her shoulder. She could feel her fingers breaking free of wiry tendrils on the other side. There *was* a hole. She pulled her arm out and began to tear the ivy away and to push herself through. Doreen came crashing towards her. She fell onto the ground on the other side and the ivy sprang back into place again behind her.

Doreen reached the spot, panting dreadfully. Bonnie held her breath.

'Wretched child!' Doreen muttered. 'Where's she gone? Oh dear, I've lost her now. Why's she got to be so difficult?'

It was a good question. Bonnie wondered too. It would have been so much easier if she'd stayed and been polite and promised to unpack her bedroom properly and said all the things they wanted her to say. Now, because of her, there was all this fuss, and Maybelle would be crying and Grandbag would say, 'I told you so.'

Doreen began to push her way back through the trees. Bonnie sighed with relief. Up above her, she could hear blackbirds singing. It was quiet now. Doreen had really gone. She looked about her. She was still in a wood. But what sort of wood was it, shut away behind high walls, in the heart of the city? She peered through the trees. There was a distant, sunny clearing. She decided to explore.

2

In the clearing, a man was digging. He paused, wiped his hot head with a handkerchief, and carried on. Behind him, a flint-faced, mushroom-shaped little house was set against the trees, its roof jutting over a wood verandah upon which languid, cream-coloured cats lay in the sun.

The man stopped. He cleaned his spade and put it aside. There was something purposeful about the way he moved, something that caught Bonnie's attention, much as the hollies had done from her bedroom window, something that made her want to know what he would do next. He began to walk towards where she was hiding. She shrank back, but he stopped without seeing her. He began pulling down dead branches and dragging them back into the clearing. Then he broke them into little pieces, crack, crack, and stacked them in the pit he'd dug, pausing now and then to wipe his forehead again, and fan away the heat of approaching noon.

Bonnie wondered how she could move closer without being seen. The man disappeared into a shed, and she thought she saw her chance, but he reappeared with a hammer and a bag of pegs. He pegged out a circle on the ground, right in the middle of the clearing. Then he dug out a second, shallow pit. It seemed to take him ages and Bonnie became very stiff indeed, but she didn't dare move. When he'd finished, he went back into the shed and she quickly stretched her limbs. He returned with a pile of cloth which he laid down carefully and spread across the shallow pit. The cloth was a strange colour. At

14

first Bonnie thought it was black as night. But when he laid it out and the sunlight caught it, she saw that it was a deep, rich blue. What could it be? Unable to contain her curiosity, Bonnie crept forward for a better view. The undergrowth rustled around her, and she stopped. But the man seemed not to have noticed. He stood, briefly admiring what he had done, and then he climbed the verandah steps and disappeared into the house.

What *had* he done? Bonnie seized her chance and scrambled forward to find out. She could see a deep trench now, between the first pit with the wood in it, and the second pit with the smoothed-out cloth. What was it all for? She looked at the wood pile and the cloth. She looked at the hammer and pegs. She felt as if she'd walked straight down the rabbit hole into Wonderland. What was happening here?

Suddenly the man appeared, all cleaned up. She flung herself flat, among the greenery. He climbed down the steps, turned without seeing her, plunged away between the trees. She watched as he came to a gate in the wall, and unlocked it carefully. The world outside rushed to greet him. Bonnie caught a glimpse of a busy street with traffic and shoppers. The man turned once to look at his garden and then he was gone. Even from her distance, Bonnie could hear the big key locking the gate again.

Bonnie got up straight away. She made for the house. 'You can't go up there,' she instructed herself out loud. But even as she said it, her feet seized the chance and she found herself climbing the verandah steps, picking her way across the wooden boards between the cats, and standing at the front door, which she expected to find locked, but was not.

'No,' she said again, and she walked straight in.

She was plunged at once into a green, leafy darkness. No sunshine penetrated the little windows and, as if to make sure it stayed that way, rambling plants grew in pots in front of them. She could smell stale coffee and tobacco. Her eyes became accustomed to the quality of the light, and she made out shelves that were heavy with books. She saw strange things on the walls, weavings, paintings, maps, photographs. She found a carved head and a string of coloured beads. She crept forward, curiously. Her voice no longer said 'no'.

She explored the shelves, one after another. There were books on the sky at night and archaeology and ancient languages, books of geography and history, science and the story of manned flight, books on birds and farming, hang-gliding and . . .

Tap, tap! She started. It was only a cream cat sliding through the front door behind her, but it reminded her that the man would come back, that she didn't have all the time she might have wanted. She turned from the books and delved quickly in the further depths of the room. She found a door through into a kitchen. She found a back room with a sewing-machine. She found the stairs leading up into darkness.

'No.' Her hand rested on the banister. 'You can't go up there.' She began to climb. Something soft and warm touched her legs, and her heart thumped in the darkness. Then a light streak of cat rushed ahead of her. Just a cat! It pushed open the door at the top, and slithered through. She saw a chink of light, heard something too. But then the door swung shut again, and it was gone. What was it? Music?

She pushed the door open and stepped across bare, creaking boards into the brightness of noon. The sound was gone. Perhaps she'd never heard it. The room was sunny and fresh, with open windows on every side. It honoured the sky, its walls adorned with pictures of the stars at night, the stages of the moon, the rising sun. In its centre, in a pool of sunlight, a telescope pointed upwards through a glass dome.

Bonnie crossed the floor to stand beneath the dome. Then she heard it again. It was her music! She looked up. The lonely piper of her dreams called her. For an instant, she had that sense of flying again, of going up through the dome as if it weren't there, into the sky. Then she stepped back, startled, and the sensation went away again, taking the split-second music with it. She shook her head. What was the matter with her? Was she fainting? Was it the heat? Had she imagined it? The boards creaked as she stumbled to a window. She leaned against it and breathed the fresh air. Something else caught her eye.

On a desk, by her side, lay an open book which had been written in, with bold red ink. Bonnie picked the book up. It was a diary. Under the day's heading, it said, 'Pits are dug. The weather is perfect. Everything is ready. Practice flight tonight.'

Practice flight of what? She turned the page back. Her heart thumped. She had a sense that something that really mattered was about to happen. Then, right in front of her, in the same red handwriting, she read, 'A thousand years ago, men knew there was a land beyond the sky. They travelled to it and they came back again . . .'

Bonnie looked up through the dome and then back down again to the sunshine on the floor. Deep, deep inside her, in that place that daydreamed wildly about things that couldn't really be, a jigsaw piece fitted into place. *Beyond the sky.* All her life long, and though she never knew quite why, she'd known there was a land beyond the sky. She'd wondered how to get to it and what it was like. Beyond the sky. Not 'in outer space' or 'in another galaxy' but beyond the sky, the way she'd always thought of it, as if it were possible to peel away the edge of the blue and pass straight through.

The floorboards creaked. Bonnie jumped. The cream cat slid away again and she remembered she was a trespasser in the house of a man who would return. Reluctantly, she put the diary back on the desk, and made her way across the room. She climbed back down into the stuffy greenness of the living-room, and out on to the verandah, and over the cats, and away into the wood. She turned once to look at the house, then plunged on to find the hole beneath the ivy, which she clambered through.

On the other side, she leaned against the wall and thought about it all. 'The practice flight tonight . . . ' 'A land beyond the sky . . . ' She pushed her way back through the hollies towards the tarmac forecourt. She was about to step out of their shade when, like strangers from another world, ancient enemies who hardly matter any more, Grandbag and Doreen appeared at the entrance to the flats. They didn't see her and climbed into their car. Grandbag pumped the engine into life, hooted a sharp goodbye and drove away. Bonnie watched them go. Then, shaking her head as she did after a daydream, she too stepped out into the sun, and set her face for home.

When she got back, it was much as she expected. Maybelle was in the bath, the place she always went when she needed comforting. Bonnie could hear her crying through the steam. She tapped on the bathroom door and said, 'Hello. I'm back.' Then she went into the kitchen and got some lunch onto the table.

Maybelle appeared in a bath towel, with a bright, red, sweating face and red-rimmed eyes. She glared at Bonnie accusingly and sat down. She picked at her food.

'Why did you do it?'
'I don't really know.'
'Mother wasn't very impressed.'
'I don't suppose she was.'
'She says I can't control you.'
'Perhaps you can't.'

They stared at each other. Then Maybelle pushed her food aside and sighed.

'Life's too short for this,' she said. 'Come on, Bonnie. Let's try and forget it. At least she's gone. Let's go out and buy that paint.'

Bonnie smiled gratefully. Maybelle got up and disappeared to get herself ready. When she returned, her face was made up and her hair was brushed and shiny. She wore a sundress and high heels. 'We'll make a home for ourselves yet, won't we, Bonnie?' she said.

Bonnie didn't answer. She was gazing out of the window at the sky.

'Bonnie?'

She turned. For all the bright dressing, there was that thin, brittle look on Maybelle's face that she always had when Grandbag was around. Bonnie knew, with sinking dread, what was coming next.

'You do love me, don't you Bonnie?'

'Of course I do.'

'I just wanted to be sure.'

Bonnie looked back at the sky. She wished Maybelle didn't have to keep asking, to be sure.

3

It was a close, stuffy night. Bonnie tossed on her bed and dreamed of fire. She half woke and lay in a flaming sweat, listening to the distant crackle and roar of the city. Her bedcovers were in a mess on the floor. Her sheet felt hot and moist. She stumbled onto her feet and into the bathroom, splashed her face and neck with tepid water, returned to open the window and leaned out.

Cars passed on the street. Somewhere below her, perhaps among the trees, a pinprick of red light flickered, something sharper and brighter than the neon of the street lights. She looked up into the sky above it. At first she thought that the stars were invisible tonight. But then, as they appeared suddenly and then disappeared again, she realized that it was smoke that was blotting them out, as it drifted through the sky.

The words of the diary came back to her. Her mind stirred. 'The weather is perfect. We'll have the practice flight tonight.' She remembered the man breaking dry twigs in the garden next door, stacking them up into a pile, and she looked back at the red pinprick of light. Not a dream fire, this time. It was a real one.

Without hesitation, she dressed and climbed out onto the balcony. It chimed four o'clock as she passed by Maybelle's bedroom window. She climbed down the fire-escape and picked her way across the tarmac and among the hollies. When she came to the old wall, she felt for the hole and clambered through. The crackling of undergrowth beneath her feet, the crunching of leaves as she pushed her way among them, seemed very loud in the hush of night. But she pressed on, too curious to care.

Ahead of her, a bonfire burned. She could smell the woodsmoke, hear its hiss and snap. She crept from tree to tree towards the clearing, and at last she stood close enough to feel its heat. She peered through the branches and saw something strange, a path of what looked at first like underground light, coming from the bonfire. Suddenly she realized it was the dug-out trench. It had been covered and the smoke and flames were rushing along it from the first pit where the fire had been made, to the second, shallow pit where . . . where what? She stared, astonished.

A dark monster bobbed with its greedy mouth over the shallow pit where the smoke came out. It staggered wildly and drank the smoke greedily, growing bigger as she watched. Bonnie suddenly recognized what it was. It was the cloth that had lain upon the ground. It had become a balloon. Huge poles on either side of it helped to hold it secure with a web of ropes across it and tethers all over the ground. It bobbed at its mooring-place, angry with the tethers, impatient to get away.

The man appeared. He was fighting with it, trying to keep it down, to keep its mouth over the smoke, to control it. As the balloon filled out, it became harder to hold. Suddenly, and from where she wasn't sure, other figures appeared. Dark like shadows, quick like flickering flames, they grabbed the mouth of the balloon all the way round, and struggled with it.

Bonnie leaned forward. What was it about those figures? She saw pale hands on the dark side of the balloon, eyes glittering in the firelight, bodies darting from side to side. And yet her eyes couldn't catch them properly. Their heads were always half-turned away. They were quick and light, like the flames themselves, like things that weren't really there. Did they all, she wondered, know about the land beyond the sky?

21

The man gave a sudden shout. The balloon was full as a midsummer moon. Its wide, open mouth glowed red with heat. It was bursting beneath a sky which began to lighten. They couldn't hold it any more. It had to go.

As they cut the ropes and the huge poles crashed away on either side, Bonnie realized, surprised, that she'd got it wrong. How had she done that? There was only *one* shadowy figure working beside the man, racing up and down in the firelight with the speed and strength of ten. One boy pulling a few last dead branches off a tree, tossing them into the last of the fire. One *boy*.

'It works,' the man shouted. 'It works!'

The untethered balloon shook free. It went straight up. Somewhere, not far away, a police siren moaned. Bonnie hardly noticed. She looked into the night sky that was turning now to morning. The balloon went up and up into it without wavering, long after the police siren had wailed away. Up and up into the early morning blue. She watched till it was a dark, lonely inkspot and her neck ached with following it.

She looked down again. The fire was burning low. The man and the boy were gone. She waited to see if they would return, but when they didn't she turned to go as well, to rustle back through the dewy grass and over the wall and across the tarmac and into her bedroom where she could play with the pieces of the jigsaw in her mind, cast about within herself for understanding.

'It was a lovely sight, wasn't it?'

He stood behind her, smoking a cigarette, the man from the house. In the early morning light, she could see his face was dark like a gypsy's and his hair was gingery brown, like a ripe nut. His eyes were grey and still and careful. Her heart thumped with the sudden shock of his being there, but she didn't run away. Surprised at herself, she said, 'Will it come back down?'

The man shook his head. 'No,' he said. 'It's too dark.'

'What?'

'Midnight blue,' he said, and then, realizing she didn't understand, 'The sun will keep the air inside hot because the cloth's so dark, and as long as it's hot enough, it goes up.'

'Oh.' She looked up again. She couldn't see it any more.

The man threw down his cigarette, stamped on it. 'Come and sit on the verandah,' he said. 'I'll get us some breakfast and you can tell me what you're doing in my garden.'

Bonnie gulped uncomfortably. He turned and walked away from her. The choice was suddenly hers, to turn and run away, or to follow after him. And yet there hardly seemed any choice at all. There was so much she wanted to know. He climbed onto the verandah and, from behind him, puffing as she caught him up, Bonnie said, 'What happened to the boy? Where did he go?'

He stopped. Turned round. There was the strangest expression on his face. 'What did you say?'

'Your friend . . .' She faltered uncomfortably. 'You know, the boy who helped you launch the thing.'

His pause was long enough for Bonnie to wonder if she'd got it wrong again, if it hadn't been just one boy, but, as she'd first thought, many.

'Sit down,' he said at last, without answering her, and turned again towards the house. 'I won't be long.'

She settled herself on an old sofa, in between sleeping cats. He came out again with a tray full of toast and fruit and hot coffee. He dumped it down on a little table by her side and pulled up a chair, so that he was facing her. He picked up a cat and stroked it lightly, indicated that she should help herself to breakfast, and sat staring at her while she ate. All the while, he ran his finger down the cat's back and kept his eyes on her face.

To her surprise, Bonnie found that she had an appetite, that his attention didn't put her off her food. She ate. He waited patiently, as if he had all the time in the world.

When she'd finished and pushed the tray away, he spoke at last.

'My name's Michael. Tell me about yourself.'

She didn't want to tell him anything. She wanted *him* to do the telling. But it wasn't a question, she realized. It was a demand and she'd intruded in his garden and eaten his breakfast, so she began. He gave her his whole attention and, to her surprise, the story blossomed. There was something about the way he looked at her, as if he could *see* what she was saying . . . She found herself telling him about living with Grandbag because Maybelle couldn't look after her, about getting their own home at long last.

'You'd like Maybelle,' she said. 'She's really fun. At least, she is when Grandbag isn't around.'

'What's she like when Grandbag's around?'

'Well, she can't make up her mind about things and she cries a lot. Things don't seem to work out the way she wants them to and she feels, well, useless . . .'

Her voice trailed off. She hung her head. Gently, Michael changed the subject.

'How did you get into my garden?' he said mildly. 'I keep it locked, you know, and the wall's very high.'

Bonnie told him about the hole in the wall.

'And why did you come?'

Why had she come? It seemed to burst from her, without her control. 'I . . . I wanted to know about the land beyond the sky. I read your diary. I know I shouldn't. I know it was wrong. I know you'll be really mad at me. But I couldn't help it. And I'm glad I did, even if you *are* mad at me. I've always known inside myself, you see, that there was a land beyond the sky.'

He stopped stroking the cat. Lit another cigarette and drew on it a couple of times.

'I'm sorry. You must be really cross with me,' she said miserably. 'You *are*, aren't you?'

He didn't answer.

'It's light now,' she said awkwardly. 'I'll have to go. I don't want Maybelle to know that I've been out. I just hoped you'd tell me how you know for sure . . .'

He got up. Threw down the cigarette. 'Come on,' he said.

'What?'

'*Come on . . .*'

He *was* going to throw her out. She didn't blame him. She should never have allowed herself to be caught. Now she'd never know . . .

'*It looks as if there's something I'll have to show you.*'

He wasn't throwing her out. He was marching across the verandah towards the house. Cats were scattering . . .

'Don't just stand there.'

She followed him indoors. He brought a big book off a shelf. It was a history of flight with a torn paper cover and yellow-edged pages.

'There are all sorts of things in here,' he said. He began to thumb through, and photos, drawings, diagrams whirred before Bonnie's eyes. 'Here,' he said, stopping suddenly and stabbing with his finger. 'I found this. It's just a little bit. Read it yourself. Most people would think it was just a story. But I *did* it. You saw me. I did it tonight. And just like the genie when the lamp is rubbed, the shadowboy appeared.'

Bonnie looked. There was a picture of a broken piece of pottery with a black balloon on it and a red fire and smoke and a soft grey shadow-figure holding a stick with which he poked the fire.

'Read it,' said Michael again. 'There's nothing new. They did it before us, a thousand years ago.'

4

Bonnie woke. She heard Maybelle's bedroom clock strike nine and she could see that it was bright outside. The door was slightly open and from the kitchen came the sound of the radio and the smell of something cooking, something buttery and sweet and not at all like the burnt toast which was all she'd ever known Maybelle to produce at breakfast time.

She sighed. She wasn't hungry. She remembered breakfast on Michael's verandah and creeping home in the early light, back through the open window and into her bed. And then she remembered the rest, the ancient secrets Michael had unlocked, of flight and more than flight, of the land beyond the waving curtains of the sky, of the shed full of more blue cloth, mountains of bigger, fresh balloon that waited for the real launch tonight . . .

Maybelle stuck her head round the door. She wore an uncharacteristic apron.

'Wake up,' she said. 'Breakfast's ready. We've got a lot to do today.'

'I'm not very hungry.'

'Don't be silly. It's pancakes. I made them specially.'

'All right, all right. I'm on my way.'

When Bonnie entered the kitchen, Maybelle was sliding pancakes onto plates. She was slightly flustered and obviously not used to such early efforts. The recipe book was propped up on the shelf beside the stove. A chaos of pans and bowls lay all around the sink. The window was open and smoke was drifting away. But the radio sang and Maybelle hummed along with it. And the pancakes were crisp and curly on the edges and soft and brown in the middle where the sugar had been sprinkled.

Bonnie sat down, found her appetite, and ate. All the while, Maybelle hovered attentively.

'You do like them, don't you? Are they warm enough? Are they nice and light? Would you like some more sugar? We could have them every day.'

When she'd finished, Maybelle said, 'Do you realize, this is the first proper day of our life together? Isn't that exciting? Come on, let's get going.'

'Get going with what?' Bonnie eyed the dishes unenthusiastically.

'With this,' Maybelle said, and she hauled the pots of red and yellow paint out of the cupboard. 'We'll get it all done today you know, if we make an early start.'

Bonnie'd forgotten all about the plan to decorate her bedroom.

'I've been waiting for this day for *years*,' Maybelle said. 'Isn't it wonderful?'

She hauled the paint down the hall and into Bonnie's room. Then she began covering everything in ragged sheets and shouting for brushes. 'Can you bring the radio?' she called, and she attacked the nearest bit of wall with big, carefree brush strokes.

Bonnie brought the radio and plugged it in. It was a hot day already and she pushed the window open as wide as it would go. Across the tarmac, she saw the hollies. They were thick and wild and she couldn't see anything of the house behind. It was hard to get excited about painting a bedroom when she thought of what would happen over there tonight.

Maybelle began to sing along with the radio. She bounced up and down. She'd already covered half a wall. There were paint spots on the carpet, but she carried on regardless and didn't seem to care.

'We'll get them off afterwards. Bonnie, take the red.

Make a start on the cupboard door.'

Bonnie found a little brush and a red pot of paint, and began. The room began to look remarkably lively. She couldn't resist a twinge of pride. 'I told you red and yellow would look good together,' she said.

They paused for lunch. They'd finished one whole coat, all the way round. Maybelle said they'd let it dry for an hour. It was so hot, it wouldn't take long. Incongruously, she started talking about Christmas plans. It was hard to imagine Christmas with the windows open and the sun beating through them.

'I've brought you a present, actually,' Maybelle said. 'I couldn't wait for Christmas.'

She disappeared into her bedroom. Bonnie heard her rustling and thumping and the bedroom clock chiming. She reappeared, looking slightly embarrassed, with a ridiculous plant in a pot, a huge thing with green, floppy leaves that fell everywhere.

'I bought it this morning,' she said, 'when I went to get the stuff for the pancakes. Isn't it nice?'

She dumped it down. 'It'll go with the yellow walls,' she said. 'I know I shouldn't have, but it *was* reduced. Perhaps if we can't afford a Christmas tree, it'd do instead. If you look after it properly, we could use it every year.'

Bonnie stared at it, knowing she couldn't possibly have afforded it. Oh, Maybelle . . .

'It's lovely,' she said.

'Put it in your bedroom,' Maybelle said. 'Let's see what it looks like.'

Bonnie tried to pick it up. It began to topple. Maybelle helped her with it along the hall. The doorbell rang. Maybelle helped her sidle it into the bedroom and then turned towards the unfamiliar shape beyond the frosted glass of the front door.

When she came back, Bonnie had shifted the plant over to the window and started painting again.

28

'You'll have to be careful not to get paint on it,' Maybelle said.

'Grandbag would tell you off for spoiling me.'

They both grinned.

'It's next door,' Maybelle said, gesturing towards the hall. 'They want to know if we'd like a cup of tea.'

'I'd rather get on,' Bonnie said. 'You go.'

'Suit yourself,' said Maybelle. 'I think I will. Get to know the neighbours. After all, we're going to be here a long time . . .'

When she'd gone, Bonnie sat on the bed and looked beyond the plant and the yellow walls and the red doors and skirting-boards. It was a relief to be quiet and on her own. Memories of last night, pushed away by the day, crowded back again. She thought of Michael's fire tonight and the big monster of a bag which he'd fill with smoke to lift him through the sky. She thought of the darting shadowboy. She thought of the inkspot in the sky — the experimental balloon. Where was it now? Had it passed through the veil, exploded in the atmosphere?

'At least we know it really can be done,' Michael had said. 'We *can*, like the ancients, send bags of smoke up into the sky.'

'I wish I could go with him,' Bonnie thought.

The doorbell rang again. She supposed Maybelle had left her key. It rang again, impatiently. It wasn't like Maybelle to be impatient.

'All right, all right, I'm just coming . . .'

Grandbag stood on the doorstep in her black-and-bead coat, with Doreen behind her, clutching a suitcase.

'Don't just stand there. Let us in.'

As if in a dream, she stepped aside. Grandbag marched past her and down the hall towards Maybelle's bedroom. Doreen hauled the suitcase behind her.

'What are you doing, Grandma?'

'What does it look like?' Grandbag opened Maybelle's bedroom door, and Doreen pushed the suitcase in. 'I've come to stay,' Grandbag said. 'I've never been one to turn my back on my children when they needed me. Doreen, put my umbrella over there. Hang up my coat. Now you can go. Don't stand around there. Don't forget to feed the bird, will you?'

Doreen slunk down the hall and outside. Bonnie's abiding final memory was of her backing, all bony arms and legs and drab print frock, along the covered walkway towards the stairs. Her voice faded as she said, and said again, that she hoped she'd manage all right on her own, that she was sure she'd be all right really, that Grandbag mustn't worry about her.'

'Silly woman,' Grandbag said. 'Of course she won't manage. She never does. I suppose she'll have to move in too. Where's your mother?'

'She's next door,' Bonnie said. 'Having a cup of tea.'

'Well, get her.'

Bonnie stumbled along the walkway to the next flat. She thundered on the door and tumbled in. 'Maybelle, Maybelle, Grandbag's here! She's come to stay! She's brought her suitcase!'

'What!'

Maybelle dropped her tea on the carpet, and there were apologies while they tried to clear it up. Then they were outside, with Maybelle, white-faced, muttering attempted parting pleasantries. Then they were at their own front door, hand in shaking hand.

'You've got to make her go,' Bonnie said. 'If you don't do something now, we'll never get rid of her. Even if we move, she'll follow us. We won't ever escape!'

Grandbag opened the door, before Maybelle could answer her. 'What have you done to that poor child's room?' she said. 'Those horrid colours, what can you have been thinking of?'

Maybelle let go of Bonnie's hand. 'I just thought. . . '

'Never mind what you thought. Make me some tea.'

Meek as a lamb, and ghastly quiet, Maybelle went

into the kitchen and filled the kettle and plugged it in. Bonnie followed, hurling piercing, desperate looks at her, which she ignored.

'If you get a move on,' Grandbag said, 'you'll have time to go down to the shops and change the rest of that paint for white.'

Bonnie gave up, turned away. She crept along the hall into her bedroom. She shut the door, sat on the bed. She stared at the plant. Her foot felt something underneath the bed. It was her little cardboard suitcase, the one she'd always kept her night things in when Grandbag had, reluctantly, let her spend odd nights with her mother. She pulled it out. She thought of Michael. *She'd ask him to take her too*. It was timed just right. As if she were meant to go.

Grandbag called her. She pushed the suitcase under the bed again. Grandbag's voice informed her that there was some shopping for her to do.

5

A cream-coloured cat rattled the window-pane. Bonnie sat up, consulted her watch, got out of bed. The flight would be at dawn, but Michael said it would take all night to fill such a big bag with smoke. She looked out of the window. The cat had gone. She could see the light of fire already, over the wall.

She dressed, crept into the kitchen and helped herself to a small, light breakfast. On the way back to her room, she paused to look at sleeping Maybelle in her bed, her face pale against Grandbag's arm, which was slung across her like a shadow. Grandbag snored contentedly. Maybelle tossed, helpless to get free.

Bonnie turned away to her own room. She made her bed and packed her suitcase as she would for staying away overnight. She looked about her, at the plant and the yellow walls and the raggedy doll that had followed her everywhere else, but not this time. Then, clutching her suitcase, she opened the window and climbed out onto the balcony and down to the ground.

The cream cat was waiting for her. It strutted across the tarmac and disappeared among the hollies. Bonnie followed it. An eruption of red, volcanic cinders rained gently down around her. Smoke filled the air. The atmosphere seemed more intense, explosive, urgent than it had the night before. Bonnie hurried on and wondered how the people in the flats could sleep through it all.

She found the wall and struggled through. The fire was enormous. It crackled and roared. Even from this distance, the heat hit her. She pushed between the trees and entered the clearing. The dark bag, too, was vast, many times the size of last night's balloon. Bonnie saw the shadowboy. He *was* one boy. If she really strained her eyes, she could see that now, although he moved like twenty. He opened the balloon's mouth wide to catch the smoke, he shook out its cloth to help it fill, he clutched it as it grew, straightened it as it toppled from side to side. He seemed to be everywhere. He seemed to have the strength and speed of a whole team of men. He wasn't an ordinary boy at all. Just what was he?

'Hey, Bonnie. Over here . . . '

Michael's voice came to her above the roar of the fire. She looked up to the verandah and he waved to her. Forgetting the shadowboy, she put the suitcase down, and climbed the steps. Michael was tying something together with rope.

'What's that?'

'It's the gondola. It'll go beneath the balloon. It's what I'll travel in.'

Bonnie touched the wicker hammock. Michael tied the last knot and threw it down. 'That's done,' he said. He looked beyond the verandah, at the balloon which towered above the tree-tops now. The shadowboy seemed to have tethered it all down. 'That's done as well,' he said. 'Just look at it!' They both watched it bounce against the ropes. 'I've given it a name,' Michael said. 'I'm calling it Midnight Blue. It looks black now, but you wait till the sunlight's on it. It'll go the darkest, richest . . . '

'Michael.'

'Yes?'

'I want to come too.'

Turning from the balloon, he saw the suitcase behind her on the ground. He sighed. 'Come and sit down.' He led her to the chairs and, sitting opposite her, eyed her gravely. 'How do you think Maybelle would feel,' he said, 'if she woke up and found you gone?'

33

'You don't understand,' she said. 'Things are different now. Grandbag's come to live with us and it's awful. It won't spoil things if I go. It won't make any difference at all. They're already spoiled.'

'But how would she *feel*?'

'Oh, Michael. Please let me come. I'm packed. It's what I've always dreamed about.'

'What would she *do* if you didn't come back?'

'I *will* come back.' She almost shouted it. 'It'll be like stories in books when people return to find they were only gone for a moment in time. Nobody misses them. It's always like that.'

He shook his head. 'Oh, Bonnie, sometimes they come back a hundred years later and everyone they knew is dead and the world's completely different. This is an experiment, Bonnie. We've never done it before. We don't know what to expect. All we know for sure is that it's *not* a story in a book.'

'You mean . . . ?'

'I mean if this were a story, Bonnie, it wouldn't matter what Maybelle thought. You could just go. But it's real life, and it does matter, and you can't.'

Michael looked up. It was getting light.

'I'm sorry,' he said. 'I really am. But the weather's right. The time's right. The balloon's ready. I've got to go now or I've lost the chance.'

Bonnie hung her head.

'You're still a part of it,' he said. 'I hope you'll be here to share it with, when I come back. Maybe we'll go together another time.' He got to his feet. 'I'm sorry. Come on. Let's fix the gondola.'

Hardly aware of what she was doing, Bonnie followed him down the steps. He dragged the wicker hammock towards the balloon. As they passed the fire, she put up a hand to protect her face from the heat and to wipe away the tears. They came close to the balloon. The shadowboy circled round it, struggling with the ropes that held it down while its grasping mouth drank the last of the smoke.

Michael dragged the gondola into place. Without the heart to help, Bonnie stood by her suitcase and watched the two of them fight to attach it to the balloon. She looked up, as she always did in times of trouble. The sky was delicate and light. Last bright star-drops melted in the morning. They called to her and she sighed. All she had now were the old daydreams, poor, empty things that would never be the same again. She lowered her sights. The balloon stood, a moon-shaped monster, bursting its cords in eagerness to get free. She lowered her sights again. The shadowboy was watching her.

'That's it,' Michael said. 'We're ready.'

It was very quiet. The struggling seemed to be over, the fire to have burned low.

'Won't be a minute. I'll just get my things.'

He ran back towards the house, up the steps and inside. Bonnie looked up at the thing which towered like a giant above the tree-tops. It was an awesome sight. She wondered if anybody out there beyond the walls looked through their windows and saw it too. And then she heard something.

The first note of it she thought was birdsong, the dawn chorus. But the second note sang out, and she knew that it was not. Then the third note rang. She knew what it was. The lonely piper called her with the slow, compelling music of the high sky.

She picked up her suitcase. Her heart thumped, but her head was clear. She passed before the fire. The shadowboy seemed to be waiting for her. The balloon towered above them both, its gondola swinging like a cradle at her side. He took her suitcase and threw it up and took her hand and lifted her in. Then he jumped up beside her, light as air, and began to tie her in. She felt his hands flickering across her body till she was secure. Then something strange began to happen.

35

'What's going on?' she asked, but he didn't answer. 'The ground's running away.'

She saw ropes hanging loose, poles falling away, tree-tops sinking beneath her. It was flight. She saw Michael on the verandah, with his bag in his hand. Then she was over the tree-tops and the flint-faced, mushroom-shaped little house disappeared between the closing trees. She could see the tarmac forecourt and her bedroom window and a flash of yellow wall. She could see the road with its street lights fading in the morning, and the tops of the shops and the roof over the flats.

As they rose, the sun rose with them, as if they were racing for the top of the sky. Its warmth welcomed them, turned the dark skin of the fiery balloon as Michael had named it, midnight blue. They flew straight up. Above them, the sweet, clear music of the lonely pipe, the only sound left in the whole world, drew them on until they prepared to hit the very roof-top of the sky itself. Then the smooth sky puckered into cloth-of-blue and drew aside for them, like curtains parting.

The music called again, and they passed straight through.

6

Arabella dangled her legs out of the bedroom window and closed her eyes. She felt a butterfly brush against her knee, rubbed her skin against the mortar and bricks, drank in the warmth of the morning sunshine on her face, her arms, her feet. She heard dogs barking down in the valley and the rumble of tractors in fields and the curling cries of Florence in her pram as she talked herself to sleep. She heard the steady pulling of sheep at the orchard grass at the side of the house, the swish, swish of footsteps through the long grass, the clicking of the little side gate. She heard the pattering of Jake's restless paws upon the terrace beneath, and opened her eyes. Mum was back home.

'Arabella, you'll fall and break your neck. I'm always telling you that. Get back through that window. What can you be thinking of, sitting out there like that?'

'I'm bored. I don't know what to do.'

'Come and help me make a chocolate cake, then.'

'Cakes are boring.'

'Come and arrange these flowers.'

'I don't want to arrange flowers.'

'I'm going to make lunch for the men. You can take it up to them.'

She looked at the valley and the hills beyond, patchworks of field that were in the midst of being harvested, all pale in the hot sun and woven together with ribbons of river and road. She looked at Mum, who removed the sunhat from her head and fanned herself gently with it.

'Oh, all right then . . . ' She began to climb back through the window.

'Pull the curtains across, will you?' Mum called after her. 'Make a bit of shade.'

She looked across the room, from the flowery curtains and the sunlight on the wall, to the bed beneath the sloping window at the back, with its crisp, white, turned-down sheets. Bright particles of dust hung immobile in the air. Last winter's ashes lay still in the fireplace. The dolls sat in a row upon the mantelpiece, ancient dolls that had belonged to Mum and Grandmother and unknown little girls before them.

She sighed. 'It's like it's all frozen in time, and me with it,' she said out loud. 'Like this is how things have always been and always will be. Oh, how boring.'

She drew the curtains and crossed the floor and paused beside the bed to look up through the sloping window at the hawthorn hedge and the meadow and the craggy white standing stones up on the top.

'Nothing ever changes.'

Down the corridor, the staircase was decorated with paintings of them all, her and Mum and Grandad and countless other similar faces that all stared out at her and reminded her, as she climbed down the stairs, that men and women may come and go, be born and die, but the family goes on and stays the same for ever. She rushed down past them all and through the door at the bottom. She found herself in the kitchen with its hissing stove, which Mum kept going even on the hottest days, and its open windows with their little breeze, and its cool flagstone floor.

'There you are. Pass me the butter. There's a good girl. It's over there.'

Mum was slicing bread. Chopping up salad. Arabella brought the butter out of the pantry and put it down on the table. Mum indicated that she should sit down too and help her.

'It must have always been like this,' Arabella sighed.

'What's that?' said Mum.

'Women making lunches,' Arabella said. 'Filling baskets with food to take out to the harvest. The stove hissing like that. The little breeze at the window. Cats all round your feet, hoping you'll drop crumbs for them.'

She sat down and began to butter the bread and Mum filled the sandwiches with wedges of crumbling cheese and thin, moist slices of cucumber. The cats rubbed their legs and waited for crumbs to come their way. Mum put the sandwiches into a large basket, with a handful of sweet red tomatoes and a small, nutty fruitcake. Then she disappeared into the pantry and brought out from the cool shelf some bottles of beer and a large, cold meat pie.

'Put these in too, will you?'

Arabella put them in. She looked up and Mum was watching her. 'I'm sorry you haven't got brothers and sisters nearer your own age,' she said. 'I'm sorry life's so dull for you. I know Florence is only a baby still, but she'll be some sort of company, one day.'

Arabella fiddled with the handle of the basket. Mum always seemed to *know*.

'I had the strangest dream last night,' she said. 'I dreamt I was lying in bed, looking up through the window. It was early, getting light. A dark, blue moon fell out of the sky and into the holly grove.'

'The holly grove?' Mum tilted her head to one side. 'I used to dream about the holly grove, when I was young. How strange.' She put the last things in the basket. 'You can take it all up. It's ready now. They might need some help. You can stay with them if you like.'

Arabella stumbled through the darkness of the scullery, with its smells of mouse and freshly chopped logs, past the old stone sink and out into the sunshine. Jake bounded up to her and wove his silky body between her legs. Arabella crossed the terrace and slipped through the gate into the orchard. She half skipped, half ran between the apple trees and long grass, scattering bees and sheep and smelling the grass and pollen and earth. Every now and then she stopped to put down the basket and rest her arms. She heard the steady mumblings of the harvester on the hill above.

'Come on Jake! That's a good boy! I'll beat you there.'

She climbed over the stile into the garden meadow and began to run again, up towards the holly grove. She could see the harvester on the field up above it, moving up and down. She could hear the shouts of men. Jake ran ahead of her. He plunged into the dark shade of the holly trees. She hesitated before following him. Put down her basket to rest again, aware that if there were any other way up to the top, she would have taken it.

The holly grove was ancient. The trees were twisted and dark, their branches tortuous. They formed a dense, gnarled ring, with a large grass-and-moss clearing in the centre. You slipped into that ring and it was as if you'd entered another world. Arabella looked at it now. Long strands of fleece hung like listless washing on a line. Last dots of pink foxglove wilted in their shade.

She struggled through onto the moss. Nothing moved. Not even a flower stirred, not a bird or an insect or the smallest leaf. Slowly she put her basket down. The buzzing world seemed to stand still with her and hold its breath. Up above her, near the top, she could see Dad on the harvester. He seemed a million miles away. She could have stood here for the rest of the day.

'Whatever's the matter with me?' Her words fell like pebbles into a pond. They rippled and then the clearing was still again. 'Whatever's the matter with me?' she said again and, despite the day's heat, she found herself shivering. 'Come on Arabella, let's get out of here. They must be starving up there. And thirsty too.'

She picked up the basket. 'I'm talking to myself again,' she said. 'Talking out loud. Mum says I mustn't do it, but she does it too.'

Dad was down off the harvester, cursing at the thing because something had gone wrong and it always happened when you most wanted it. Mr Onions was trying to tell him what to do, and Ned and Henry were trailing across the field, delighted with the chance to stop work, and full of advice.

Mrs Onions appeared over the top, with her husband's lunch. She, like the rest of them, lived beyond Roundhill, down in the cottages at the back. A small cat followed her. It rushed away in fear when Jake came bounding up.

'Well, Jake, you rogue,' she said. 'Look what you've gone and done.' She pulled his ears playfully and ran her hand down his back. 'Where's that girl of yours?' she said. Jake pulled away from her, as if he didn't have the time to waste. 'I beg your pardon, Jake. What's the matter with you?'

Dad lifted his head out of the engine. 'What's the matter with who?' he said.

'With Jake,' Mrs Onions began, but Dad was staring past her. She turned, and Arabella was running up the field towards them all.

'Dad! Oh, Dad! Help!'

They all ran. Jake bounded ahead of them. He leapt and wove his way through the harvest. Dad followed on his heels.

'Dad! Dad!'

She fell into his arms, face all shiny and out of breath. He held her tight. The others came up behind.

'What is it? What is it?' Mrs Onions said.

Arabella's breath came back to her. She pulled herself out of Dad's arms.

'You've got to come,' she said. She turned to Mrs Onions too. 'You've got to come right away.'

'Of course we will.' said Dad. 'But what is it?'

'There's a girl,' Arabella said. 'Down in the holly grove. She's just lying there. She's dead.'

7

Bonnie drifted into and out of sleep and the clock ticked, and it comforted her. Gradually, she became aware that she lay in a large bed, that her head was supported by a soft pillow smelling of roses, that light, crisp sheets rustled around her as she moved. Through a haze she heard voices, but her eyes were too heavy to open and she couldn't see who spoke.

'Will she be all right?'

'Poor little lovely.'

'Good job Arabella found her.'

'What's wrong with her?'

Then she heard Maybelle's voice. 'I don't really know what's the matter with her. She seems exhausted and I think she may have had a knock, but I can't find any bones broken. I think we ought just to keep her quiet and let her rest . . .'

She fell asleep again. She felt safe, comfortable now. The clock ticked. It was the clock in Maybelle's bedroom. She felt the golden glow of sunshine on her face. But what had happened? As her mind drifted away, she saw a huge balloon falling through the sky, a world rushing to greet her, ropes, a swinging gondola, a boy's face leaning over her . . .

She woke again, briefly. The sun had moved round. The tick of the clock was louder and closer. She struggled to open her eyes and stared at the tulip motifs carved upon the base of the bed. They meant she wasn't home after all, for this wasn't Maybelle's bed. She'd never seen this bed before. Where was she?

'Will you be all right with her now? I've got to go and get Mr Onions' tea. Is there anything else I can do before I go?'

Bonnie struggled to find the person behind the voice but her eyes would not stay open. She drifted away, and in her dream she thought she heard Maybelle again.

'Don't worry, Mrs Onions. I'll be all right. I'll sit with her a while. Michael can manage downstairs.'

When Bonnie woke again, the clock was striking nine. She opened her eyes. The room was dark. She lay still, gradually taking things in. She'd never been inside a room like this before. The ceiling sloped above her, criss-crossed with black, craggy wooden beams. It sagged, and the walls bulged and plaster crumbled off them, revealing bits of ancient stone. Beyond the bed, an old black hearth reminded her of the row of antique shops in the road behind Grandbag's flat. There were china dogs upon the mantelpiece and books on shelves.

Suddenly, over by the open window, a seated figure moved. Bonnie started. It had been so quiet and still, she'd not known anyone was there. Her bedcovers rustled, but the figure didn't seem to notice. It looked up at the sky. There was something about it . . .

Then the head moved slightly, tilted to the side. Bonnie recognized the gesture. She stared through the moonlight of this unknown room. It was Maybelle's way of tilting her head, Maybelle's way of resting her shoulders, Maybelle's chin now on Maybelle's hand.

What was Maybelle doing here?

'Hello, Mum. Is she all right?'

Bonnie's skin went cold all over. Why could she hear her own voice, when she wasn't speaking? The figure at the window turned. It was Maybelle's face too, but she wore a cotton, tightly-buttoned, rosy nightdress which Maybelle never would have worn, and her face was tired.

'Yes. She's all right. She's only sleeping. She'll be fine

in the morning. Have you fed those cats yet, Arabella?'

'Not yet. I'll do it now. I . . . I can't help wondering if
we'll be friends.'

Bonnie's heart thumped so loud she couldn't believe
they didn't hear it. She moved her head slightly, carefully, anxious that neither of them should know she was
awake. Who was it who spoke with her voice? Through
slits of eyes she stared towards the doorway. A girl stood
there, shining in the moonlight. Bonnie bit her lip so as
not to cry. She was staring straight at herself . . .

Up in the holly grove, it was dark now. Sheep rustled
among the dusty roots. Up above the circle of spiky
branches, a first star shone with a light that seemed to
call from other worlds.

The shadowboy slithered under and between the
holly branches and out onto the hillside. Night animals
carried on their business all around him. Owls swooped
over the roofs of the farm buildings below him. Bats
above him chattered in the evening air. Mice ran along
hedgerows. A thin, light-footed cat stalked its prey.

The boy began to pick his way down the meadow.
The navy sky was filling with glassy bits of stars. He
came down at the back of the house. This was where
they'd brought the girl. To one side of it was a fenced
orchard with a little stile and sheep paths that snaked
up from it onto the hill. To the other was a farm gate
and a yard and the barns. He crept down to the gate.
The grass beneath his feet hardly rustled as he walked
over it. The birds and animals around him moved as if
he weren't there. He swung his thin, pale body over the
top bar, slunk gently into the yard. A side door opened,
throwing a patch of yellow light onto the terrace that ran
right along the front. A figure appeared.

'Come on . . . come on . . . come on . . . '

It was a young girl with yellow hair. Her hands were

full of dishes of food and she rattled them together and called again.

From out of the barns and the long grass of the meadow and under the gate as if he weren't there, from along the terrace and over the yard and from the orchard on the side, the farm cats appeared. The girl put down her bowls and disappeared. She returned again with a jug of milk. The cats miaouwed and lapped and rubbed themselves against her legs and lapped again and she laughed at them all.

'Arabella, get a move on. You ought to be in bed.'

'All right, Dad.'

Out on the yard, the boy heard the door rattling shut. The cats continued to lap. The boy looked right across the valley at the little dots of other farmhouses that brightened all the time, as the darkness grew. He slithered across the yard so quietly that not a cat turned to see who was there, not a cat noticed as he slid the latch and slipped into the barn.

There was fresh grain waiting for the merchant to come for it, and bales of straw, and hay. The smell of the place nearly overwhelmed him. But, like the hillside animals, he too had a job to do. His feet tiptoed forward. He heard rats scampering in corners. His hands felt their way along the straw until he felt something that did not prickle, that did not crack beneath his touch, something soft as a woman's dress, handfuls of the stuff.

He held it up before his face. It appeared as black as night. It was the balloon, laid out upon the straw where they had put it when they'd brought it down from the hill. His hands crept over it carefully, felt the fine, strong weave. When he was satisfied that it wasn't torn, he felt and checked the ropes. Then he reached beyond the ropes and found the wicker gondola. It all was there.

Suddenly there was a din outside. The shadowboy crept to the door. Something dark was running across the yard. He peered between the cracks in the barn

door. Agitated owls swooped and shrieked and fluttered. Shrieks of distress came from the henhouse. The
side door was flung open and a man appeared. The boy
heard a shot ring out. He saw the fox, with a broken,
mutilated chicken in its mouth, escape away.

'Blast!' the man shouted at his failure. He went back
in and slammed the door.

The shadowboy slithered out into the yard again.
He'd done what he came to do. With the gun's explosion
ringing through his head, he began to follow the fox's
trail, back up the hill. He followed it up the sheep's path,
back through the holly grove and over the half-harvested
top meadow. He followed it over the stone wall and
among the bracken and whinberries and wild rambling
heather of the top. Then the path divided. One way led
to the white stones on the very top. The other led to a
lower, softer, bulge of a hill.

The fox climbed this lower hill and the boy followed
him. They started down the other side. The fox knew its
path well. In the darkness the shadowboy saw a cluster of
cottages, tucked in beneath the brow of the hill. He crept
towards them. They were bleak, brave little places ringed
with rowan trees and hawthorn hedges and crumbling
stone walls. Smoke drifted to greet him. Yellow dots of
lights shone out of windows. An old man sat out in the
porch of the first cottage, cleaning his garden tools. A
woman appeared round the side of the cottage, from her
own henhouse.

'Have you shut 'em in?' the old man said. 'Fox is out.
I seen him running by.'

'Course I have. I wouldn't let him get 'em,' she replied.

'It's a grand night,' he said, looking up at the sky.

'I wonder how the little girl's doing?' the woman said.
'I wish they'd brought her back here. I'd like a little girl to
nurse.'

The old man laughed. 'Silly woman. You've got *me* to
nurse.'

'You, Onions, *you* . . . '

'And the cats and the hens and the sick hare and the hedgehogs and that silly fat sheep of yours.'

Laughing, they both turned back into the house. 'I'll get us a bite of supper,' the old woman said.

'That'll be nice. Harvesting makes me awful hungry, all the time. Do you know, I think it's turning chilly.'

They shut the door. The shadowboy wondered what it must be like to be a person, to need to eat to stay alive. He wondered what it was like to feel cold, to want to close yourself indoors, away from the great, wide, open sky. It was different for him. He never felt cold. He never felt tired. He didn't have a lifespan. He did what he had to do.

They were strange things, people.

8

It was light when Bonnie woke again. The chair by the window was empty. She was alone. She sat up. A dressing-gown had been thrown across the counterpane, and she plucked at it and wrapped it round herself. She got out of bed and began to explore, first the half-opened wardrobe with clothes peeking out of it, then the mantel-piece with its plants and ornaments. Her little cardboard suitcase leaned against the dressing-table. She turned to pick it up, and then she saw, on the dressing-table top, a silver frame with a photograph of Maybelle and herself in it.

'I don't understand.'

She said it out loud and a cream cat jumped off the bedside chair and ran away. She leaned across the dressing-table and picked it up and stared from it to herself reflected in the mirror, and then back again. The clothes were different, and the hair. But it was enough alike to make her shiver.

'I don't understand.'

She remembered the woman in the chair and the moonlit girl in the doorway. She turned her head and there was Maybelle's clock, Maybelle's own bedroom clock, ticking its way towards the chiming of another hour. She shivered again and dropped the photograph back quickly where she had found it, and crept away from it, towards the door. Where was she, and what was going on here? She opened the door and half expected to find the hall to Maybelle's flat on the other side of it, to hear the radio's murmur in the kitchen, Maybelle crying in the bath, Grandbag shouting crossly from the bedroom that she wanted her early morning cup of tea.

But it was a strange world on the other side of the door, a dark, heavy-timbered, stooping, sagging corridor with doors off it on either side, the sort of place you only ever read about in books.

'I feel like I'm Alice,' she whispered to herself. 'I haven't gone down the rabbit hole, but I'm surely dreaming, all the same . . .'

She began to creep down the corridor, pausing carefully at each doorway in case boards squeaked. She came to the staircase. The walls were full of portraits that bore her likeness.

'I *am* Alice,' she thought. 'This *is* Wonderland! Who *are* these people . . . ?' She turned nervously away from the paintings and followed the corridor to its end. In the dark she saw a flight of narrower, more tortuous stairs. 'I wonder what's up there?' she said. She began to climb and, as she did so, she remembered another flight of stairs, another day, the flint-faced house, the room with the glass dome at the top.

Her progress was halted by a hatch. She pushed, and it slid open. With ease she climbed, not into a light and airy room, but into the stuffy darkness of a long, low attic full of packing cases and tea chests, old books and bits of furniture and rolled-up carpets.

At the far end sunlight filtered through a sloping roof-light. She padded towards the light, just able to stand straight beneath the ridge beam. The floor was uneven and in places it was broken. She stooped down and looked through one hole into the bedroom where she'd slept. Then she looked through another hole. She could see coat-hangers and clothes and a wardrobe door that was half open and a corner of a bed beyond, with a sleeping girl in it.

Getting up again, she peered out of the window. The

roof sloped down and there was a flat bit with a wall around it and she thought, 'What a great place to hide!'

She pushed the window open, showering her face and hair with dust as she did so. Then she slid out onto the roof, slithered down onto the flat bit, leaned over the wall.

A fresh breeze gently stirred her hair. She looked up into the sky. It was streaked with orange sunrise stripes and the clouds were pink. She looked down. The valley was pale with morning mist. She'd never seen such an empty landscape. No houses, no cars, no kids on bikes, no shops or buses.

Suddenly the ground seemed to come up at her. She thought, 'It's a long way down there,' and felt giddy. She turned back towards the sky-light and began to scramble in again. The attic was warming up for the day. The air was still. She felt as if she couldn't breathe properly, began to pick her way back carefully between the holes in the floor . . .

And then she saw something. What was it? An open box on the top of a tea chest containing a coil of wooden beads. She'd seen them before. She was *sure* she had. She picked them up and then she saw the bits of telescope beneath.

'Hello.'

A sun-tanned face with nut-brown hair poked up through the hatch.

'Michael,' she said.

'Yes?' the head replied. A body scrambled up after it. It *was* Michael. He looked at her with grey, still eyes.

'What . . . what are you doing here?' she said.

He smiled. 'That's just what I was going to ask you,' he said. 'There's really nothing to see up here. Do you want to come down and get some breakfast?'

She stared at him. He didn't seem to know her. 'The telescope . . . ' she said.

'I never use it,' he said. 'Don't know what to do with

the thing. Are you feeling better?' He peered at her through the gloom, as if she were a perfect stranger. 'You certainly seemed to need that sleep.'

'Y-yes,' she said. She put the beads back down. 'I'm much better now.'

He stood, head bent beneath the ridge of the roof, running his fingers through his rumpled hair. 'We were quite worried about you for a while, you know,' he said. 'Mum said she thought you needed rest. She sat with you. You couldn't have been in better hands.'

She looked at him through the dusty air.

'You ought to have some breakfast,' he was saying. 'You don't, if you don't mind me saying, you don't look . . . quite recovered yet.' He wore workman's overalls and shabby carpet slippers and his hands were pitted and dark, like well-worn tools. Michael's hands were like that too, but this man was different from Michael. She couldn't explain how. He wasn't the man who'd watched her escape in his balloon. Just as the Mum wasn't really Maybelle and the girl wasn't herself.

'We'll show you round after breakfast,' he said.

'W-where are we?'

'Highholly House,' he said.

She'd heard the name before . . .

Arabella woke excited and didn't know why. It was the same bedroom as usual. Nothing had moved, nothing changed.

Why was her heart beating so fast? Why did she have that birthday feeling, as though there'd be presents at the breakfast table, cards on the mantelpiece, a cake waiting in the pantry?

Then she remembered. There was a strange girl in Mum and Dad's bed. She'd come out of the sky. That falling, blue .moon hadn't been a dream, it had been a huge balloon. A strange girl . . . Mum said, if she was better today, she could show her over the hill. Mum said maybe they'd be friends. At the thought of it, Arabella's excitement shrivelled to awful, ordinary shyness. It was a lonely life on Highholly Hill. She didn't know how to make friends.

'I'll go and see if she's awake. I won't *talk* to her. I'll just peep at her through the crack in the door. I don't *have* to talk to her if I don't want to.'

She got out of bed, struggled into shorts and T-shirt and tiptoed to the room next door. She pushed the door till she could see through the crack. The bed was empty. Suddenly, awfully, she thought, 'Something's gone wrong. She's run away or died in the night.'

But then she heard a burst of voices below her in the kitchen. The stair door swung open as a cat pushed its way through. Breakfast bacon smells rose to greet her. And everything had to be all right. Mum would never be cooking breakfast and singing and laughing if the girl had died or gone away.

Shy again, she climbed down the stairs. At the bottom, she pushed open the door.

'Ah, there you are,' said Dad. 'Awake at last. Come and meet Bonnie.'

He took her hand and led her in. The girl was sitting at the table picking at her food. She nodded at her, feeling foolish. She couldn't think of a thing to say. The girl nodded back. She was fair-haired, pink-cheeked, pale-skinned like herself, maybe her own age. Arabella sat down opposite her. The girl lowered her eyes. Arabella realized that she was nervous too.

'She's shy like me,' she thought.

Mum brought her some breakfast. 'Eat it quickly, won't you, Arabella? Then you can show Bonnie round.'

Arabella cast Mum a silent, appealing look for help. But Mum ignored it. She turned her attention to Florence, who was agitating for her feed. The girl looked at her again. It was a strange, searching, awkward stare. She seemed to take her in from head to foot. She looked now at her hair, now at her eyes and nose and mouth, now at the way her hand lifted her fork.

'What's so strange about the way I look?' Arabella thought. 'Why's she staring at me like that?'

She pushed her food around her plate and stared back at the girl, who looked away again. Neither of them could think of anything to say. The silence, as they fiddled with their food, became uncomfortable.

'I can't show her round the hill. I won't know what to say,' Arabella thought. She put her plate aside and followed Mum into the pantry where she looked for jam.

'Couldn't you come with us too?' she said. 'You know the stories about the hill. You know everything better than I do. I don't know what to talk to her about.'

'You know it all as well as I do,' Mum said. 'You'll think of things to say, don't worry.'

'But she makes me feel uncomfortable. I don't know who she is,' Arabella said.

Mum looked out of the tiny pantry window up the back of the hill. 'It doesn't matter who she is,' she said. 'The thing that matters for now is that she's what you wanted. Isn't that exciting? She's what you wanted and she's here.'

Arabella frowned. 'I don't understand.'

Mum turned away from the hill and looked at her again. 'I know what it's like to watch the still dust hanging in the air, and to be lonely and to think that nothing's ever going to change. I know what it's like to want a friend.'

Dad pushed his head round the pantry door. 'Mr Onions is here,' he said. 'I'm off. I'll see you later.'

He kissed them both and disappeared, calling good-bye to Bonnie and slamming the kitchen door behind him.

'When I first met Michael, I was too shy even to speak to him,' Mum said. 'It's hard making friends at first, but you'll be all right. Shyness goes away. Now stop making a fuss, and get out there.'

They did the house first. Arabella showed Bonnie the dusty living-room with its inglenook fireplace full of cob-webs and dried flowers.

'We hardly ever use this room in summertime,' she said.

Bonnie stooped and peered through the cobwebs. Benches were fixed to the wall on either side of the hearth. A great beam held up the weight of the chimney-breast. A mantelpiece sagged beneath plates and candle-sticks.

'Mum says chimneys were always built first,' Arabella said. 'If you got your chimney up in a day, then the land you built on was yours.'

Bonnie hardly heard her words. She'd never seen

such an old house. She stared up at the criss-crossing of oak beams above her head. Arabella crossed the room and opened a door which led into a lighter room. 'This is where I have my school lessons.'

'You mean you don't go to school?'

'It's so far down to the village. You wait and see. It's just impossible getting in and out in winter, unless you walk. Mum was taught up here too, when she was a girl.'

'But what about other children?'

'Other children?'

'Don't you have friends?'

Arabella shook her head and looked uncomfortable. 'I see people when we go down for the Bank Holiday Show and when we have our harvest supper or go to market. But it takes so long getting down and there aren't any other children up here any more. Mum says the cottages at the back of Roundhill used to be full of families. They worked up here and over the back in what used to be the mines. Mum says all the children used to come for school here. But now there's only me.'

'It must be *great*, not going to school.'

'It does get lonely . . . '

They worked their way back through the kitchen and along the upstairs corridor. Arabella paused at the attic stairs. 'There's nothing up there,' she said. 'Just an attic, and the floor's not safe. I'll show you our bedroom.' She led Bonnie on to the room at the end. Bonnie looked at her suitcase on the bed.

'Mum says you can sleep in here with me,' Arabella said.

They stood side by side, their reflections caught in the dressing-table mirror. 'Don't you think,' Bonnie said nervously, 'that we look a bit . . . the same?'

'A bit, I suppose.' Arabella peered at their reflections.

'You don't . . . you don't think we look *just* the same?'

Arabella looked at her curiously. 'We're the same height. But no, not really. Why do you ask?'

'Oh, I just wondered . . . '

They came down the main stairs. 'We never use the front door,' Arabella said. 'Or the hall.' She opened a door at the back of the hall. 'This is the last room you haven't seen. This is Mum's sewing-room.'

They stepped into a neat, little sitting-room with flowers in vases and velvet curtains tied back from tall french windows and a beautiful treadle sewing-machine, inlaid with mother-of-pearl. A dressmaker's dummy was half-draped with a calico frock. In a corner sat a spinning-wheel, beside a basket of oily fleece. A couple of sinking armchairs were set before a shiny, tiled fireplace.

'It's Mum's special room,' said Arabella, making for the french windows. 'She spins in here as well as sewing, and knits us sweaters by the fire in the winter. You can shut your eyes and almost feel that she's here. Come on. We'll go through here. I'll take you up the hill now.'

They climbed up the garden meadow, behind the house. The holly grove loomed closer. Long strands of fleece shook like bony, white fingers in the breeze. Bonnie stared. It reminded her of other, different hollies somewhere else. 'What *is* that place?' she said.

'It's the holly grove,' Arabella replied. 'It's where we found you.'

Bonnie pictured the trees between the tarmac fore-court and the old wall. 'More hollies,' she thought. She followed Arabella up and into and across the grove. The air in it was hot and still. The breeze had died but Bonnie shivered.

'Are you all right?' Arabella said.

'I . . . I feel, oh I don't know . . . like someone's *watching* me,' Bonnie replied.

'I feel like that sometimes, as well,' Arabella said. 'I usually run as fast as I can.'

They both broke into a trot, only stopping, breathless and hot, half-way up the top field. Arabella led Bonnie through the gate onto the open hill. There were no more fences and walls, no more cultivation. The sheep's path led them up through a mass of bracken and heather, brambles, which were heavy with green berries, and whinberries.

'What's that?' Bonnie asked. She stared at a decrepit, broken sign that said DANGER! KEEP OUT!

Arabella pulled away the brambles behind the sign to reveal the dark mouth of what seemed to be a cave. 'It's called Batholes,' she said. 'There used to be mines. I told you, didn't I? They say the passages come out up here. I'd *love* to see what lies beneath this hill, but no one'll come with me.'

She looked at Bonnie almost hopefully, but Bonnie was looking above Batholes, at the standing stones on top of the hill.

'And what are those?'

'We call it Edric's Throne,' Arabella said. 'There's a smooth stone in the middle of it. It's like a seat. You can sit up there and see everything. It's the highest point for miles around.' They began to climb again. 'It's very old,' she said. 'Mum says it's the oldest bit of the hill.'

The sheep's path divided. 'That's Roundhill,' Arabella said, pointing away from the stones. 'Over the back's where the cottages are. Some of them are ruined now. The Onions live down there, and Ned and Henry. This hill's Highholly Hill.'

'Highholly Hill, with Edric's Throne on top of it,' said Bonnie. She stopped and looked down upon the farmhouse roof and the smoking chimney between trees.

'Look,' Arabella said. 'You can see why I don't go to school.' She pointed out the long snake of a track that started at the farm gate and wound its way down between the fields and hedges towards a distant cluster of roofs and a church spire. 'It's terribly steep,' she said. 'And so *long*. It goes down into the Dingle. Do you see? It's very rough down there. And then it goes over Hope Brook, up the other side, and all the way down there.'

Above them, a skylark sang. 'This is the quietest place I've ever been,' Bonnie said. 'I've never been on a farm before. I've never been anywhere so . . . empty.'

'Sometimes you can hear the hill humming,' Arabella said. 'If you listen carefully.'

They both listened. All Bonnie could hear was Dad's tractor somewhere on the hill.

'Come on,' Arabella said. 'Mum says I'm not to take you on to the top. She says I'm not to tire you. Let's go down to the barns.'

They picked their way down, down, down to the side of the house at last, where Arabella led them over the stile into the orchard.

'Do you see that there?' she said. 'It's blocked up now. It used to be our well. We have mains water now, but we didn't even used to have electricity. The well water was wonderful. It's a shame it's blocked up. Dad did it when Florence was born. He said it wasn't safe.'

She led Bonnie through the gate onto the terrace. They both looked across the yard, at the barns. 'Come and see where we've put your balloon,' Arabella said.

Bonnie hadn't expected it. You could tell that from her voice. 'My balloon,' she said. 'You've got my balloon?'

'Of course we have. Don't just stand there. Come and see.'

Arabella unbolted the barn door and led the way in. It took a minute, in the musty light, to see anything clearly, but when they did, there was the balloon, spread-eagled upon the straw. The ropes hung loosely down it. The gondola lay on the ground.

Bonnie pushed past Arabella. She took up hand-fuls of the material and held it as if it were a distant memory from another world. Arabella watched her curiously. From across the yard, Mum's cool, fresh voice cut through the heat and mustiness of the barn.

'Arabella, Bonnie, lunchtime . . .'

'We'd better go,' Arabella said. 'Mum'll be cross if

we're late.' She heard the tractor in the yard, and men's voices and Jake's bark. She made her way back to the door. 'We can't afford to waste time when we're harvesting.'

Bonnie put the cloth back on the bales. Together they came out into the sunlight. Suddenly Arabella realized she wasn't shy any more. Mum had been right. It had gone away. She looked at Bonnie, by her side.

She's not shy, either. We're *both all right*, she thought.

'We could go up the field after lunch,' she said. 'Help them, if you'd like.'

10

The sun climbed down the sky and the hill cooled. Up on the field, the workers carried on, but Bonnie crept away from them. She followed the teatime shadows along the bare ground behind the harvester and down the meadow. There was so much to think about, so many questions, so many feelings . . . Above, Mum saw her go. The silky dog began to follow, but Mum called him back again. She heard her say, 'No, Jake,' as if she knew she wanted to be alone. The harvester began to whirr again. By the time she reached the back of the house, it sounded very far away.

Mum's french windows were open. Bonnie slipped between velvet curtains into the shade of the sewing-room. As she moved through it, different smells rose up to greet her. Here tea roses, here polish, here sunshine, woodsmoke from the ashes of the fire, the earthy dankness of unspun fleece.

She stood in front of a mirror on the wall. 'Why don't they ask me who I am and where I come from?' she asked herself out loud. 'I don't know how I'd tell them — I don't think I *want* to tell them — but they seem to take it for granted that I'll stay. My suitcase is unpacked. My bed's made up. No questions asked.

'Why can't they see I look like Arabella? And like all those people in the paintings down the stairs? Why *do* I look so much like them, and why've they got the same clock in the bedroom, the same cream cats, the same telescope and holly trees, and even the name of the house?

What *is* this place? Why did I come here?'

She thought of the balloon falling through the sky, of it now, out in the barn. The shadowboy flickered through her memory. The shadowboy. Of course. 'Where are you?' she said. 'You must be here somewhere. You brought me here, you must know where we are. Surely you can explain?'

She looked about the room as if she expected the boy, having been remembered, to appear. But he did not. 'Perhaps you've done your job and gone,' she said. Would he come back? Would he take her home again? She didn't know. She didn't know *anything*.

Wearily, she sank into an armchair. Tucked down the side of it, she found a bag of knitting. She pulled it out and held it on her lap and imagined Mum sitting in this chair, knitting through the winter afternoons. Suddenly, briefly, she imagined Maybelle too. Maybelle in this pretty room, with its french windows and velvet curtains, with its decorated sewing-machine and spinning-wheel and sinking, lazy chairs. Oh, how she would have loved a husband and a new baby and a big, old house and Mrs Onions, to help her with the things she had to do.

'Poor Maybelle, life's not very fair.'

Above the mantelpiece, a painting of a man and woman looked down at her. Their hair gleamed and their clothes foamed about them like fairy wings and their jewels glittered. They sat on white horses beneath a haloed moon. Bonnie stared at them and forgot Maybelle. She wondered how she hadn't noticed them before.

'Hello,' said Mum. 'Don't let me disturb you. I've just come down to make some thermos flasks of tea. We're going to carry on while it's light.'

She stood by the french windows, shaking straw out of her hair and fanning herself with her sunhat. Jake padded past her, looked up into Bonnie's face and wagged his feathery tail. Bonnie stretched out a tentative hand and Jake allowed himself to be stroked.

'He likes you,' Mum said. 'You're honoured. He doesn't often make new friends.' She looked up at the painting too. 'Do you like it?'

'What?' said Bonnie. Jake rubbed his head now against her leg.

'My painting,' Mum said. 'You were looking at my painting.'

'Oh, I think it's great.'

'I like it too. My grandfather painted it. Michael doesn't like it much. That's why I keep it in here. It's rather sentimental, isn't it? Hardly a farmer's painting.'

'Who are those people?' Bonnie said.

'That's Wild Edric.' Mum crossed the room and pointed. 'And she's the Lady Godda.'

'Wild Edric?' said Bonnie. 'Of Edric's Throne?'

'That's right,' said Mum. 'You can see it in the background.'

'Who *is* Wild Edric?' Bonnie said. 'Who's the Lady Godda?'

'They're supposed to be the guardians of our hill,' Mum said. 'The old miners used to say they could hear them knocking in the darkness under the ground. They live down there, you see. Only come out to sit on the Throne when it's covered in clouds. Or when the hill's in danger and they've got to warn us. The story goes that the thunder roars and the lightning cracks and the very hill itself shakes when they appear.' She smiled. 'We say they keep us safe up here,' she said. 'All these years, just the one family . . . We say they keep us on this hill.'

Bonnie thought of the family faces in their frames on the stairs. Just the one family . . . 'You've always been here, then?' she said.

'Arabella doesn't know what it is to live anywhere else,' Mum replied. 'And nor do I and nor do any of us.'

A pang of envy shot through Bonnie. She thought of the times she and Grandbag had moved house. She thought of the new home she'd just left, like all the others. How could she explain her life to these people who could never understand?

'You don't have to tell us where you come from,' Mum said unexpectedly. 'We'll never ask, you know. You'll find this isn't like anywhere else you've been. You're safe up here. We're glad to have you with us. If you've come, it's because we need you. Edric and Godda always give us the things we need.'

You're safe up here . . . It was as though the whole world had been spinning, and suddenly everything stopped still and the ground was firm. 'You talk . . . ' Bonnie said, quite unable to express her true feelings, 'you talk as if you believe Edric and Godda are really down there somewhere.'

Mum smiled. 'I'd like to,' she said. 'It's a nice idea, isn't it? But I've never seen them. I like to think my grandfather must have seen *something* to paint a picture like that. But lots of people look for Edric and Godda and never see them. Do you want to sit here on your own, or would you like to come and help me make some tea?'

They made up sandwiches and put them in a basket. Mum filled the thermos flasks with tea and Jake rested beneath the kitchen window, watching them. Mum hummed to herself. She wrapped a fruitcake in a napkin and put it in the basket too. She took a pie off the pantry shelf and put it in the oven and said it would be cooked and ready when they came down. Harvesting, she said, was very hungry work. 'All food and fields and nothing in between.'

They climbed up the hill again. 'You mustn't strain yourself,' Mum said. 'You mustn't do too much. It is your first day up and about. If you're tired you must go straight back down.'

Bonnie promised that she would. Mum began to talk again.

'It's nearly time for the Bank Holiday Show,' she said. 'We always work like mad to get the harvesting done, so we can go. It means a lot when you don't get off the hill much. There are sideshows and stalls and prizes for everything. We wouldn't be able to enjoy it if half the harvesting still had to be done. This can be a bad month for summer storms. You just *have* to work when the weather's good . . .

'and talking of storms,' she said, 'I hope we get finished soon. *Something*'s on its way.'

'How can you tell?'

'It's too still. Look across the valley. It was crystal clear all afternoon, but now it's soft and mellow.'

Bonnie looked, but she could hardly take it in.

'This is me,' she thought. 'Climbing this hill with this thermos in my hand. Me, belonging in this strange, amazing place and looking for the signs and talking about weather. Me, being made welcome, with no questions asked . . . ' She looked at Mum and she wanted nothing but to be Mum's own girl, to share the hill with her for ever, to make this magic place her own.

'We thought you were never coming.' Arabella ran down to greet them. 'We're starving for food and panting with thirst.'

Her face shone with husks of grain and sweat. She grabbed Mum's arm and pulled the basket towards her to see what it contained. 'Fruitcake! That looks wonderful. And Bonnie, oh what a great sight, you've got some tea . . . '

She slid between them and slipped her arm in Mum's. They climbed the last few steps as a threesome and stopped in the shadow of the harvester. With Arabella's eager help, Mum began to distribute tea.

Bonnie woke in the night and couldn't remember where she was. Then she saw Arabella moving across the floor like a little ghost in a long white nightdress, and she knew. Arabella was crying. She stared at her. In the shadows of the night, in the same nightdress and without all the tiny, subtle differences, it was like looking at herself crying. How many times had she stood looking just like that?

'Arabella, whatever's the matter?' Mum stood in the doorway in her dressing-gown. Arabella ran to her.

'I had a dream,' she said.

'It's this awful weather,' Mum replied. 'It's too hot and still. There's no air. Quiet now, you mustn't wake Bonnie.'

She led Arabella away and shut the door after them. Bonnie lay for some time, waiting for Arabella to return, but she didn't. At last, and not knowing quite why, she climbed out of bed, crossed the room, opened the door. There was not a sound anywhere. Mum's and Dad's door was ajar. She crept up to it, peered around the side of it.

They were all asleep. Mum and Dad, and Arabella between them. Mum's hand was in Arabella's hair, Dad's arm across her body. The moon lit their faces.

Bonnie went back down the corridor. She got back into bed and stared at the cold comfort of wide-eyed china dolls and teddy-bears with glassy eyes. She shut her own eyes, but even in the dark she could see the three of them in the bed together, and she thought, 'Every good thing I've ever wanted is here and my place in it all is hers because she's their daughter.' And a feeling came over her, one that she'd had this afternoon when Arabella took Mum's arm and again before that, in a faint whiff, when they'd first met over breakfast. It was just like, well, just like she felt when she thought of Grandbag. Just like hate.

'I didn't just run away from Grandbag,' she thought, 'I ran away from *hate* . . .'

It was one of those bits of self-revelation that hits you as you drift off to sleep and you wonder if you'll remember in the morning. How could she not have known? It was the monster that had towered like a dark balloon above her head for years. A monster with a red and fiery mouth that drank people's sadness like smoke to make it grow, to fuel it till it had the strength to carry them away beyond their will to choose where they would go or what they would do.

. . . And if she hated Arabella, what would it make her do?

11

Arabella was up in the barn, watching Dad stacking bales, when Bonnie went down the yard and out onto the track.

Dad looked up as the gate rang shut. The day was horribly hot and close. He wiped his shiny face. 'Where's she off to?'

A shadow fell across Arabella's face. She picked at her dress which already, even in the morning, stuck moistly to her.

'She woke up and she was coming up the hill with us again and we were laughing about something,' she said. 'I can't remember what, but suddenly she said she'd changed her mind. It was as if she'd remembered something. I know it's silly, but she frightened me. She said she wanted to be on her own so I . . . I came down without her.'

'It takes time to make friends,' Dad said. 'It'll take time for both of you. You must be patient.'

'I stopped feeling shy,' Arabella said. She climbed down off the bales. 'And then I thought it was wonderful. But now, oh I can't explain. There's something about her . . . '

'Open the top gate for me, will you?' Dad said.

Bonnie sloped down the hill as fast as she could. She had to put as much distance between herself and Arabella as possible. She felt as if her heart would break with bitterness but she had to do it now, quickly, before she changed her mind. She realized, miserably, that she'd left her little cardboard suitcase behind, but she couldn't go back. The track twisted and turned. It seemed to take the longest and most tortuous route down to the road and Bonnie decided to cut across the fields. Sheep ran away from her. She passed right down one field, climbed over a stile, picked her way down another. She found herself where the track bent round again and dipped into what Arabella had pointed out as Hope Dingle.

The Dingle wasn't the little clump of trees Bonnie had seen from above. It dug down deep. Trees rose up on either side and leaves hung limp in the airless morning. As she scrambled down into the twisty canyon, Bonnie heard the tinkling of the brook. The track here was deeply rutted. It was stony, where great slabs of the base substance of the hill rose above the softer covering of earth and grass. She began really to understand why Arabella didn't go to school and why a once-a-year Bank Holiday Show was such an event. It was difficult getting off Highholly Hill.

The track twisted again and the white wooden sides of a narrow bridge stood out against the dark banks on either side. Bonnie clattered over the bridge. Briefly she thought of climbing down to the water below, to bathe her sticky, hot body. But if she paused, she'd think. She'd ask herself where she was going, what she planned to do.

She climbed up the crumbling track out of the Dingle, on the other side. The banks folded back. Finally, she was clear of trees. The valley lay below her, close and clear. She could see the main road and houses in the village and tractors and harvesters in the fields up on the other side. She could see a garage with a petrol sign and cars.

'Now where shall I go?'

The track looped again. She scrambled into another field and despite the sticky heat, began to run. If she followed the hedge line down, she'd be on the road long before the track finally got to it. She came to a stile, got over it, stumbled through the next field and was near enough to the road to hear every rumble of a milk lorry as it went by. She plunged into the trees that made a boundary to the field, expecting to squeeze out the other side of them onto the road itself. But they were thicker than she had expected. Once she'd dragged herself in she couldn't find the way out again. Low branches scratched her legs. She couldn't hear the milk lorry any more. She pushed her way on and saw yellow, stormy sunshine ahead of her. She wiped the sweat out of her eyes, made the last effort and got through.

'Oh . . . !'

She wasn't by the road after all. She was up the hill again, just below the holly grove, with the house below her and the skeleton stones of Edric's Throne above.

'But I *can't* be . . . !'

She had no sense of having climbed back up again, no sense of having struggled so far through the trees. She couldn't be up here. She must be imagining it. Or had she dreamed she'd climbed down the hill? Had she been here all along, just thinking about doing it?

'But I went through the Dingle. I crossed the brook. I couldn't have imagined all that.'

She got up. Her legs felt very weak. A voice inside her seemed to laugh, 'You can't escape. You can't escape.' And she remembered Mum saying, 'We say he keeps us on this hill. All these years, just the one family . . . '

She began to push herself back down the hill. She found it hard to breathe. The air was so close. She ran down past the house and the farmyard and through the fields and through the Dingle and over the bridge and down the track this time, so that there couldn't possibly be more mistakes. She was hot. She was exhausted. Round and round the loops in the track she went — and then she stopped. The farm gate stood ahead of her and the yard just beyond and the house beyond that.

73

'But it can't be . . . !'

It was.

'It can't be . . . !'

The sky was yellow and stormflies stuck to her skin. Sweaty tears rolled down her cheeks and she put up a hand to wipe them away. 'What's wrong with this hill? Why won't it let me go?' She looked up at the white stones that dominated everything.

'You'll find this isn't like anywhere else you've been . . . ' That's what Mum had said.

She sat down in the ditch beside the gate. It was too hot for crying, but she did it all the same. She wanted someone, Edric, Mum, the shadowboy, to sit down by her side and explain. But no one came. She thought of getting up and doing it all again, slowly this time, carefully. But she couldn't bear for all of it to happen again. And it would, it would . . .

She climbed over the gate, into the yard. She dragged herself up to the house, which was empty, and stood in the kitchen waiting for Mum and Dad and Arabella to return, arm in arm and all together. Jake stirred himself from his place beneath the kitchen window. She held his head and looked into his eyes.

'Oh Jake, I tried to get away. I did. What will happen now?'

12

Mum woke up. The curtains were blowing about. The room, which had been so still, was full of hot wind.

'What is it?' Dad stirred from the depths of sleep.

'The curtains,' Mum said. 'They woke me up.' She got up and closed the window. 'What a horrid wind. There's nothing fresh about it. Do you know what I mean, Michael? It's hot and sticky. I feel so hot and sticky.'

Dad grunted. Mum climbed back into bed. 'It wasn't just the curtains that woke me. I don't know what it was. It was something else.'

She curled her body up, close to Dad's. 'Jake would bark if something was wrong,' he mumbled.

'I suppose you're right.'

'Go back to sleep.'

'Perhaps I will . . . '

Arabella woke with her head full of dreams of thunder crashing in the sky, lightning ripping like an earthquake along the ground. Her heart beat fearfully. She had a horrid, full, frightened feeling in her chest. Somewhere out beyond the hill, real thunder murmured. She tried to laugh at herself.

'Fancy getting in a state because a storm's coming!' She fell asleep again.

Bonnie woke to the sound of thunder. She got out of bed and peered over Arabella's sleeping body, out of the window. The wind was up and the sky was alive, a patchwork of clouds round a moon that was first bright and then hidden, and then bright again. She watched the shadows come and go upon the landscape. She saw Edric's stones shine like white bones. She saw — right in the midst of them and while the thunder mumbled again — saw something dark move . . .

Clouds swooped down. The scene was lost. The thunder died away. 'He sits there when the clouds come down,' Mum had said, 'when the thunder roars and the lightning cracks and the very hill itself shakes.'

'I'd like to know why I can't get off this hill,' Bonnie thought. 'I'd ask him to tell me that, if he existed.'

She climbed back into bed. It must have been a sheep, up there on the stones. She closed her eyes.

And then the hill shook. It was like lightning cracking right through the ground. It was like an underground train beneath the very hill. It was as Bonnie imagined the first shake of an earthquake would be.

'If he existed . . .'

She leapt out of bed and pulled on her clothes. The hill shook again, this time gently. She tiptoed past Arabella, who never stirred, and along the corridor and through the silent house. Down in the kitchen, Jake got up and followed her and, when she got outside, she was glad of his company, for the wind was loud and the hill was unwelcoming and the thought of climbing alone, especially through the holly grove, was chilling despite the heat of the night.

They climbed up together, ran across the holly grove, tripped through the shaven stubble of the top meadow, clambered over the gate onto the wild brow of the hill. Here she stumbled through bracken. Long fingers of cloud swooped down for her and she couldn't see the moon at all, or Edric's Throne. She heard distant thunder again. Jake cowered by her side.

'Come on,' she said. 'Come on, Jake!' He wouldn't move. The cloud swirled around them both. 'I'm walking

76

into a thunderstorm,' she thought. 'And I *could* go back. My bed is warm and empty and I could go back . . . '

But then she heard something. Something different, something special. Was it just approaching thunder, or could it be horses' hooves? She tilted her head. With the din of the wind it was hard to hear. It came and went again. It could be thunder. Or it could be the hooves of Edric and Godda's horses, as the shaking ground evicted them onto the hill.

Jake shivered against her legs. She touched his warm fur, glad of his living presence by her side. The noise merged into the other creaks and groans of the night and they stumbled forward again. The cloud was thick about them now and the sound was completely gone. The path became stony. Bonnie tripped and fell and got up again. She carried on. Crashed into something . . . Pulled herself off it and saw the sign. DANGER! KEEP OUT!

It was Batholes.

She pulled aside the nest of brambles and barbed wire and peered into the cave's mouth, remembering Arabella's wistful declaration that she'd love to go down there. 'I never would,' she thought. 'I'd never shut myself away from the sky.'

She imagined the mouth cracking open into an eerie grin to let its riders out. She searched the ground for horses' hoof-marks, and found none. Perhaps it had been thunder that she'd heard. But the shaking beneath the house . . . ?

The clouds above Batholes cleared. Bonnie looked up. For a brief moment she saw the hilltop and Edric's Throne looming over everything, like a giant ghost. 'Come on Jake,' she said. 'That's where we're going.' He pressed his body unwillingly against her legs, but still followed her as she set off. She turned and touched him. 'You're a great dog, Jake.' And then she ran.

The stones of Edric's Throne towered above them.

Bonnie had never thought they'd be so thick and wide, so fortress-like. She stopped to get her breath back and then, resolutely, began to walk around their outer edge, looking for the way in to that smooth stone at the heart of them, where she'd seen . . . What *had* she seen?

'There's surely no such person as Wild Edric,' she thought, for now she was up here the whole thing seemed absurd. 'I won't find horses' hoof-marks. I won't find anything.'

She put out her hand and touched a stone. It was cold as death itself. Then she saw a long, dark entrance between the stones, a black, jagged finger that seemed to point a way in. Her hand slid into this crack. She let it lead her on, holding it out in front of her like a pale, fluttering butterfly. The dark was all around her now. She was in a pitch-black corridor, with stone on each side. She followed the guidance of her pale hand. She heard the wind somewhere outside. Her crushed body was frozen now and she couldn't believe that the night, the wind, the hill had ever been hot. 'This,' she thought, 'is what it's like to be a fossil. If the stones moved, even slightly, I'd be entombed for ever.'

But they didn't move. The passage opened out and spat her, unprepared, onto the smooth white stone where Edric, hidden by clouds or mist, was meant to brood over his domain.

The Throne was empty. A full blast of the approaching storm knocked her back, so that she almost fell. The wind whistled like an angry ghoul through cracks in rocks and out the other side of them and over the top again. Jake tumbled out after her and lifted his head, sniffing the angry air. She stepped forward, wrapped by cloud so that she could hardly see, and he rushed in front of her, blocking her way.

'What is it, Jake?'

She stepped forward again. He howled. And then the cloud briefly thinned and parted and she saw that she was standing on the edge of a chasm, with only Jake between herself and the fields far below.

'Oh . . .'

The wind blew at her. She could hardly stand up. She wanted to get away, but she couldn't move. The cloud swirled between her and the land again. It was as if long, white fingers of rumbling storm reached out for her from a cloudy cauldron that was awful in its emptiness.

'Oh, Jake, oh . . . !'

The lightning cracked, above her head. Jake's ears flattened and he let out a low, demented yell. In her panic to run away, to squeeze back between the rocks and onto the open hill, to find herself once again among growing things, bracken, hawthorn hedges, grassy meadows, orchards, Bonnie turned. The wind got hold of her. It tottered her towards the chasm. She began to fall.

And then a pair of arms reached out and grabbed her . . .

13

They ran over stones and down through furious, shaking bracken. Bonnie stumbled and fell and the shadowboy pulled her up and dragged her on. She cried and the wind lashed her hair across her face, so that she couldn't see where she was going. Jake wove a path around them, and the boy stumbled over him and they all fell down. The storm was overhead now. It was so close you could reach out a hand and almost drag it down.

'Get up,' the boy said. 'Come on. Quickly.'

'I can't.' Bonnie gasped for breath. 'I can't go on.'

'Yes you can. Come on.'

'I *can't*.'

He dragged her down to the edge of the holly grove. Behind them, Edric's Throne was electric and alive with livid, greenish lightning. Everything was suddenly illuminated. Thunder crashed right over their heads. Jake howled. The boy got Bonnie from behind and pushed her straight into the tangle of holly leaves, down on the ground among the earth and roots and last late foxgloves. She screamed. Her face was scratched, her hair was dishevelled. He caught and pushed again and they were through. The three of them rolled onto the moss in a great ball of sweat and skin and arms and legs and fur.

The ground was soft. The grove was very, very still. It could have been a moonlit midsummer night with not a blade of grass stirring and a faint sheen of dew on the moss. Out on the hill, the storm roared on, but the grove . . . Inexplicably, the grove was safe. Bonnie sat up. She didn't hate the holly grove any more. Her breath came evenly again.

'You saved my life,' she said to the boy. 'I don't know how to thank you.'

She reached out her hand. He looked down at it, all heavy and hot and human, and drew back as if her touch might make him cumbersome and earthbound too, as if it could contaminate him with — what was it — humanity? She didn't seem to notice. She put her hand on his arm and he felt the weight of it, even through his sleeve. On top of the hill, the lightning cracked again.

'If we'd still been up there,' she said, flinching, 'it would have struck you and me.'

He shook his head. 'Not quite,' he said.

'What do you mean?'

'It wouldn't have struck me.'

She let go of him. Beyond the grove, sheets of rain fell, loud as thunder, out of the sky. She drew her knees up to her chin and hugged her legs and, ignoring the storm, tried to make the boy out. He seemed to flicker as she looked at him. He seemed to come and go. She remembered thinking he was twenty men. Even now, she could understand why.

'What *are* you?' she said, cautiously.

'I don't know,' he answered.

'You're not a person, are you?'

'People feel the cold,' he said with distaste. 'They feel the heat. They're heavy and solid and they get wet in the rain. They can't get out of themselves. They can't stop *feeling*. Their feelings make them *do* things and then they're not free.'

'You think you're free?' Bonnie wanted to laugh, but what he said had touched her somewhere, all the same. 'You're just a genie in a lamp. Someone digs the right pit or makes the right balloon, and you appear.' She got up.

Shook off his words. Looked away from him, around the hollies.

'What do you know about this hill?' she said.

'Nothing,' he answered simply again.

'But you must know where we are, why we came here? I can't get off. I've tried you know, but I can't.'

He shook his head. 'I'm sorry.'

'You brought me here,' she said. 'Not just anywhere, but here. Don't you even know how long we'll be here?'

'No.'

'You don't know much, do you? You're not as different from me as you'd like to think. And you must have feelings. Everyone has feelings. Don't you get lonely?'

It was a stupid thing, but he remembered the fleeting touch on his arm.

'I'm lonely,' she said. 'I've got everything I could ever want, and I don't belong. You must get lonely too. Out here all on your own, not knowing where you are or why you do the things you do.'

'Of course I don't.'

But she wasn't listening any more. At least not to him. The rain stopped and the wind softened and she turned her head. Her whole body stiffened.

'What's that?' she said.

He listened. He heard something too, but it was hard to be sure.

'Horses' hooves!' she said. 'Can't you hear them? Down there by the house.' She moved away from him. It was all quite sudden. 'I've got to go. You see, I came up here to find . . . ' and she was gone, running down the sheep's path and through the lower rim of hollies. 'Thank you,' she called again, 'for rescuing me.'

He looked around him. The holly grove was shadowy and grey and still and lonely now. *Lonely* . . . She'd planted the word and now she'd gone.

'I wouldn't want to be like them,' he said. 'Always *wanting*, always *feeling* things.'

But her human hand had touched his arm and his words sounded thin and hollow.

The hill was sodden and the grass flat. Battered branches littered the ground like the debris of a major disaster. Bonnie squelched and stumbled her way down the meadow. Her ears strained for the sound of horses' hooves again. The sky was clearing and she stopped and looked all around her. Rainwater tinkled in rivulets down the field. Whatever she had heard was gone, and the noisy wind was gone as well, both disappeared like a conjuror's rabbit back into its hat. Gone!

Dejectedly, she made her way down towards the house, over the stile, into the orchard. She threaded her way between the fruit trees and Jake scrambled after her. She hardly noticed him, because something shimmered like a dewy spider's web between the smallest finger branches of a distant apple tree.

What was it? She walked on and it grew brighter. In the dark orchard it seemed to have a light of its own. She stumbled over the stones of the covered well. It was right above her now. She squinted and reached up and took it in her hand. Everything, the storm, the shadowboy, horses' hooves, Wild Edric and the Lady Godda, even her own plight, were momentarily forgotten.

It was a silver chain, with a glittering flower pendant hanging from it. Jewels were set in the chain like a string of stars. Bonnie cupped her hands around the flower, spread out the chain, touching it, stone by stone. It was hard to see what they were in the dark. Were they diamonds? Were they rubies or emeralds? They were so light, and yet she'd always thought that real jewels were heavy and solid and weighed you down. She turned it over. Its clasp was a tiny pair of silver hands.

She slipped it round her neck and joined the hands together. She fingered the flower as it settled over her blouse. She'd found a treasure and she felt like a queen.

Jake stirred impatiently. Jewels meant nothing to him and it was getting light.

'All right. I know. Come on.'

She tucked the necklace underneath her blouse and buttoned it up, right to the neck.

'Whose is it?' she thought. 'Why was it hanging in a tree? I hope it's not something Arabella's lost. She's got everything. I want this to be mine.'

She crept down to the orchard gate. It creaked as she opened it and she stopped and looked up at the front windows, but no lights came on. She tiptoed along the terrace, past the living-room window, past the bulge of the kitchen, round the side to the scullery door. A pair of silvery eyes glinted at her in the first glimmers of dawn. She stifled a scream. Then Dad shifted slowly from one foot to the other. He was leaning against the kitchen wall.

'Good morning, Bonnie.'

'Oh. You made me jump. I never saw you. You frightened me.'

The last of the moon shone on him and he looked so much like Michael that she couldn't believe, just for a moment, that he wasn't. Then he drew on his pipe and nodded down into the valley in only Dad's way.

'They're getting ready for the Show,' he said. 'I thought the storm would ruin it, but it's cleared up now. It'll be all right.'

Bonnie followed his gaze. Tiny lights were moving up and down. A Land Rover throbbed. A pale marquee fluttered in the midst of hammering men.

'Never can sleep,' Dad said, 'before the Show.'

Bonnie looked again. Tractors squelched. Lamps bobbed on long poles. She heard voices, carried in the clear air. Dogs barked and cocks crowed.

'Is it a fair down there?' she said. 'Swings, big dipper, roundabouts . . . ?'

'That's right,' said Dad. 'And there's the judging marquee for the home produce. And the pens for the animals. And the ring . . . '

'You'll be going?'

'We always do.'

'Can I come too?'

'Why ever not?' Dad looked from the distant fields to the wet, rain-sodden yard and then to Bonnie. 'What a strange thing,' he said. 'You're not wet at all.'

Before she could think what to say, he tapped out his pipe and stretched himself.

'Don't know about you, but I'm cold and stiff. I'm going to make breakfast. It's nice eating early. It sets you up for the day. I hope you're not going to make a habit of wandering off up the hill in the night . . . '

Bonnie sat out on her own. Dad had gone. The kitchen light shone onto the terrace. She hardly noticed it. Jake sat by her side. She hardly noticed him. What would happen if none of them could get off the hill? If they *all* finished up in the yard again, or up by the holly grove?

She looked down at the bustle in the valley. Tents were springing up like August mushrooms in the field. She fingered the necklace beneath her blouse. It chafed slightly against her skin, and there was something about those tents that chafed her too. What was it? She couldn't explain, even to herself. The boy's words came back to her. 'Feelings make you *do* things and you're not free.' And she thought — what made her think it? — 'I could do something really terrible. I know I could. It's why I ran away from Grandbag. I could have killed her. People read in newspapers about children doing things like that and they can't believe it's true. They think it's all made up. But I could have. I *still* could . . . '

Oh, she was tired. She'd been out half the night and she'd thought and felt and done and seen so much. She got up to go in, and then she noticed Jake. His ears were flattened. His body was stiff and still.

'What's wrong with you, Jake?' she said.

He stared down at the valley. He didn't move.

'You're tired too. Silly dog. The storm's over now. Everything's all right,' she said. But he still didn't move. 'You can stay here if you want to, but I'm going back to bed.'

14

There were four bars. It was dark and there they were, yes, four of them between Bonnie and the door with the strip of light under it. She reached out a hand. Why was it so small? Why was it so hard to reach the bars? She stretched and wriggled and at last got her fists round them. They were so large. It was difficult to hold them. She tried to pull herself up. Her legs felt weak. It was hard to stand. What was wrong with her? She heard footsteps outside. They came closer, closer.

Then she knew. This was a dream. She'd dreamed this bit before. She was a baby in a cot but it was only a dream, she was all right. She didn't need to struggle, to be afraid. Still locked in the dream, her tiny legs gave way. She fell onto her back. The door opened and the light clicked on. *It was all right.*

In the dream room two beds faced each other in the corner, discarded clothes heaped all over them. A chest of drawers stood between them with nappies piled on top. She saw a dressing-table with a pair of tights over the mirror and pots and packets of make-up and bottles and brushes scattered everywhere. Next to the dressing-table a metal, painted desk was cluttered with piles of magazines and pens and homework books. Above it, a poster was tacked onto the wall. A school uniform was draped over a chair.

Two girls came in. The girls who shared her room. The thin, nervous one she didn't like, the soft, pink, nice one who played with her. The thin one sat before the mirror. She fiddled with her hair and unscrewed the pots and made up her face. The pink one sighed.

'I wouldn't do my hair like that,' she said. 'And the make-up's all wrong, you know. Oh, I wish I was as old as you. I wish I could go out.'

'Well, you can't,' the thin one said. 'You've got to do your homework.'

'But I never have any fun.'

'You know what Mother said.'

'It isn't fair.'

'Oh shut up, Maybelle. Life isn't fair.'

'You don't always *have* to be mean. You'll be sorry for it one day.'

'I wouldn't want to be soft and wet and kind like you. If you don't get on, I'll tell, I will.'

The pink one settled reluctantly at the metal desk. The thin one pulled a limp, grey, sagging frock over her head, frowned with dissatisfaction at herself in the mirror, and went out. As soon as she'd gone, the pink one came over to the cot and poked her soft, warm fingers through the bars. She leaned over and lifted Bonnie out and held her close against herself.

'Doreen can have her going out. Least I've got you. I love you, Bonnie, love you, yes I do.'

The door opened.

'*What* do you think you're doing?'

'Oh, Mother . . .'

A black-garbed, solid woman pounded across the room. She removed Bonnie from the soft arms and put her back behind the bars. Her voice was cold and angry.

'I've fed her,' she said. 'She's meant to be asleep and you've got work to do. Haven't you wasted enough of your life already? You'd better come downstairs where I can keep an eye on you. You're not to be trusted. You'll never change. Come on. Downstairs.'

The pink girl held the side of the cot.

'I'll have her one day,' she said in a low, shaking voice

that even a baby could recognize as frightened. 'I won't always be too young to make a home for us, you wait and see.'

The woman's eyes glinted. 'You're such a fool,' she said. 'God help her if you ever had her to yourself. You're useless, Maybelle. Useless.'

'I know I'm useless,' the pink girl said. 'I know I've made a mess of things, but . . . '

The woman wouldn't wait for any more. She whisked up the school books from the table, took Maybelle's arm and propelled her sharply through the door. She turned off the light and shut the door behind them. Bonnie heard their footsteps fading. She was on her own again. She began to cry. She wanted the pink girl to come back and play. Nothing happened and she cried louder. She didn't like the dark.

Suddenly the door reopened. It was the woman again. She didn't turn the light on this time. She came across the room like a fast, black shadow. She leaned over the cot and this was the moment . . . this was the moment when Bonnie knew it wasn't all right, that she didn't want to dream this dream. It wasn't all right at all . . . She struggled to wake and couldn't. She struggled to get away from the woman and couldn't. She stopped crying. It dried up somewhere inside of her. She shuddered instead. She couldn't stop shuddering.

The woman in black reached out a hand. She had such a big hand and the skin was so hard. She thrust a bony, pointy finger into Bonnie's side and began to tickle her with it. Only it wasn't a gentle, friendly tickle that comes in play. The finger prodded ferociously. Bonnie squirmed. She tried to get away from it, but she couldn't. Then the face leaned over her, closer and closer. She could see right inside the mouth and smell the breath. 'I've brought you up this far,' she whispered. 'You're good as mine. Don't think I'll *ever* let you go.'

Bonnie saw a small, wet dribble trickling down the woman's chin.

'No, Grandbag, Grandbag no!'

The words screamed inside her head. Then the bony finger tickled her again and she screamed out loud this time and the mouth was laughing . . .

Bonnie sat up. The bed was wet. She could feel it underneath her in a warm patch. She clambered out and surveyed the patch in horror. It was ages since she'd done that. But it was ages since she'd had the dream. She dragged the sheet into the bathroom, rinsed it out, dragged it back into the bedroom and hung it over a chair in the sunshine. It was only a dream. It wasn't real. She mustn't get upset. She looked around her. Reality was sunlight bursting through curtains and pretty dolls in a row over the fireplace and rugs on shiny oak floors. It was Arabella's empty, neat bed. It was Arabella . . .

She heard laughter at the breakfast table downstairs. Arabella's excited voice rose above the others. Oh, everything would be all right if it weren't for wretched, stupid Arabella. She began to dress. All the thoughts, all the things that had happened, whirled, mad as last night's storm, inside her head. She stood before the mirror. It was hard to believe that such a still, quiet face hid so much turmoil.

Then she saw the necklace. It chafed her neck and she tried to get it off. The clasp wouldn't undo. She twisted it round and looked at the clutching silver hands. There seemed to be no point where they joined. She twisted it round again. In the light of day she saw sky-blue enamel between the dots of diamond stars, and a lump of smooth, fantastic gold right in the centre of the jewelled flower. She laid the thing back against her neck, looked at it in the mirror. It reminded her of something. What was it?

'Bonnie!' Arabella's head poked round the door and

Bonnie thrust the necklace underneath her shirt. 'You must come down now. It's nearly time to go.'

Go? Of course, it was the Bank Holiday Show. Arabella's face was bursting with impatience and excitement. Bonnie buttoned her shirt.

'All right. I'm ready. I'm just coming.'

She followed Arabella downstairs. The kitchen was an uncustomary mess of pots of jam and pickle and flowers and vegetables in baskets.

'Ah, Bonnie,' Mum said. 'I've left your breakfast on the side. Be very careful not to knock the chocolate cake.'

She wore a best dress and a hat and high-heeled shoes. Bonnie stared, surprised, and she laughed. She was poking flowers into a china vase.

'What do you think?' she said. 'Will I win the flower arranging?' Before Bonnie had time to answer, she whisked them away. 'Arabella, will you clean Florence up?' Her voice trailed back to them through the darkness of the scullery. 'Her fresh frock's by the stove . . .'

Arabella got Florence ready. Mum trekked back and forth. Bonnie ate, and when she'd finished she dropped her bowl in the sink and went outside to where Mum's careful packing in the back of the Land Rover was nearly finished. Over by the barns, Dad was securing a trailer door. Something inside the trailer made its protests heard.

'That's Bess,' Mum said, looking up. 'She's the best cow we've ever had. She's bound to get a prize. That's a nice necklace you're wearing. Where did you get it?'

Bonnie looked down. The top buttons of her shirt had popped open. The necklace looked splendid in the sunshine and she felt like a thief. She flushed. Mum's eyes were full on her.

'I . . . I found it,' she said.

'Oh?'

'It was outside. In the orchard. I . . . I hope it's not yours. Or Arabella's?'

92

Her face was lit up bright. 'It's very fine,' Mum said, as if she hadn't noticed. She looked at it with thoughtful eyes. 'It's not ours. But I'm sure I've seen it before. How strange to find a thing like that out here . . .'

'Can you drive the Land Rover back?' called Dad. 'I want to hook on.'

'We'll talk about it later,' Mum said. 'Like Arabella says, we mustn't be late.'

She jumped into the driver's seat, fancy hat and all, and reversed to the trailer which Dad hooked on. Then she made back for the house and Bonnie was left on her own, trailing up and down over broken bits of branches from the night before.

The air was clear but she didn't feel the way she usually did when a storm was over and things were fresh and safe again. The necklace chafed. She had an awful, sinking, quiet sense, almost of doom. She looked down at the white marquees and remembered Jake, with his ears drawn back and his stiff body. Then she thought of her dream. Why had she dreamt it now?

'Out of the way, Bonnie. That's a good girl.'

Dad moved her aside and climbed up into the driver's seat. Mum appeared with the girls.

'The necklace,' thought Bonnie. 'I know what it reminds me of. Of course.'

'I won't be a minute,' she said. 'I won't be long.'

She rushed back up to the house, through the big door which nobody used, and into the dark front hall. The sewing-room door was open. She entered and stood in front of the fireplace and stared up at the painting. There it was, Godda's necklace, sparkling down at her! She fingered the jewels around her neck, the blue enamel, the diamond stars, the flower with the golden heart . . . What did it mean? They were the same.

15

'I wish she'd hurry up,' Arabella said.

'Here she comes,' said Mum.

'Mr Onions went an hour ago,' said Arabella. 'I know nobody goes as early as him, but all the same . . . '

'We'll be all right,' said Dad, and he opened the door. Arabella moved across and Jake slithered under the seat. Mum put Florence on her lap and Bonnie squeezed in.

'All right?' said Dad. 'Then off we go . . . '

'I'm sorry I kept you,' Bonnie said.

They drove along the hill. It was a fine day, so clear, now that the storm had gone, that you could pick out every tree on the hill opposite. The track plunged down towards Hope Dingle and Arabella shivered excitedly as the showground grew bigger before her eyes. She could see the main ring with bales all round it, and the cattle pens. She could see the flags. They lurched into the Dingle. Dad slowed the Land Rover right down. They tipped and turned and Dad eased them over the little bridge.

'You'll have to get out here,' he said. 'It's going to be a bit of a job getting up the other side.'

Once they were out, Dad forced the engine forward again. They climbed up the track behind him. Mum took off her high-heeled shoes. When they came to the top, Dad was waiting for them. Bonnie, Arabella noticed, hung behind. She was pale and quiet. She fiddled with the collar of her shirt.

'Come on,' Arabella called. 'We don't want to miss anything.'

They rolled down into the village. It was spread out in front of them, a cluster of rooftops and a spire and the tops of yew trees in the churchyard. Arabella noticed Bonnie's hands, clenched together nervously. The track turned into a proper, made-up road, with cottages of brick and stone on either side. They passed a farm and a pub. White, dotted lines appeared in the middle of the road and they saw a road sign and a telephone box and a yellow AA sign that said TO THE SHOWGROUND.

'We're down!' whispered Bonnie, as if she was surprised. Arabella frowned, puzzled, but Bess mooed as if she understood, and Jake's head poked out from under the seat.

'That's right,' said Dad. 'All in one piece. That's not bad going. That track gets worse and worse. We'll have to do something about it one of these days.'

'Is my hat all right?' said Mum. 'I hate the silly thing, but everyone wears them.'

They crossed the main road, past a garage on the corner with a row of petrol pumps. Dad steered them onto the end of a queue of Land Rovers and trailers, all much like their own. At last a steward directed them in through the gates, and Dad drove up behind the large white marquee.

'We're just in time,' he said. 'Let's get the stuff out, and I'll go and park.'

Mum and Arabella began to unload. Jake jumped out and raced round and round. Bonnie stood and stared and Arabella wondered what she was thinking. There were crowds everywhere, boys on motorbikes, teenagers with headphones on, the smell of hotdogs wafting through the air . . .

'Come on, Bonnie,' said Dad. 'Put those flowers over there.'

'Be careful,' Mum said. 'Put them down gently.

Arabella can you get those carrots? That's right. Oh, Bonnie, can you grab Florence? She's got the chocolate cake . . . '

Dad got back into the Land Rover and drove away.

'Can I leave you with Florence while we take things in?' Mum said to Bonnie. 'We won't be long, and we can't take her with us. She'll wreck the place. Can you look after Jake too? They won't want dogs in the showing tent.' She thrust Florence into Bonnie's arms and filled Arabella's with flowers and cake.

'Come on, come on,' Arabella said, hopping from foot to foot. 'We'll miss the judging.'

'No we won't,' laughed Mum. 'We're right on time.'

She followed Arabella, tucked her arm in hers. 'I want to find the man who sells boots. Remind me, will you? I really think we'll win the flowers this year. Here we are. Come on, 'Belle . . . '

Bonnie held tightly onto Florence. Jake looked up at her. The minutes dragged by and the others didn't come back. Bonnie turned away. The words 'Come on, 'Belle . . . ' rang in her head and she thought, 'I don't belong with them. It doesn't matter how hard I try. I hate that wretched hill.'

'Shall I have Florence, then?' a voice behind her said. She turned and Mrs Onions, resplendently attired in best suit and pink net hat, held out her arms. 'You're only young once,' she said. 'You didn't ought to stand round here. Go off with you and enjoy the Show.'

Her body seemed the perfect shape for holding babies. Bonnie willingly let Florence go.

'Take this,' Mrs Onions said. 'You won't get far without money.' She handed Bonnie a new, bright pound coin.

'Thank you.' Bonnie took the coin and Mrs Onions smiled.

'It gets awful noisy,' she said. 'I don't suppose you

96

young ones think so, though. I'll take Florence to the tea tent. It's nice and quiet in there. To tell you the truth, I don't much care for the Show.'

'You can almost smell the straw on her,' Bonnie thought, as Mrs Onions went away. 'Straw and earth and animals . . . ' Behind the tea tent, she saw the distant silhouette of Edric's Throne, against the sky. She turned away from it, from the tea tent, from Florence, Mrs Onions, Mum, Dad, Arabella. From them all. She had decided. 'I've got away this time. I'll never go back up there.'

She pushed her way through the crowd. There were mums and dads and kids and gangs of teenagers with candyfloss and stallholders selling wares. She stumbled onto the nearest ride, the bumper cars. The music screamed and the cars crashed until she'd had her money's worth. She got off and bought a hotdog and covered it with mustard and, not knowing where she was going or what she would do next, she started to look for the way out of the showground.

Suddenly the necklace began to hurt again. She stopped and undid buttons and rubbed her neck.

'I wish I'd never put the wretched thing on,' she said, twisting it round and trying to undo it. It stung her more and she pulled it angrily. She didn't care if it was precious any more, or how she'd found it, or if it really had been Godda's. She didn't want Highholly Hill and the legend of Godda and Edric hanging round her neck for ever more.

She put her hand up to her throat, clutched the flower pendant and pulled as hard as she could. For one awful moment her hand stuck. A terrible pain jerked through it, up her arm, into her shoulder, into her head itself. It was like an electric shock. She cried out, and 'No!' said the pain. 'No. You can't get away from me. There's danger, danger and I'm warning you. You've got to notice me.'

Suddenly, everything seemed unpleasant and sinister. She pushed through the crowds again, through the shrieking voices on every side, between the sea of jostling faces. A tall man with a dark face and the blackest eyes leaned towards her and shouted 'Come and have a go, two goes for 50 pence.' She turned her back and ran away from him and wished Jake was still by her side. With the memory of pain imprinted from brain to hand, she turned a corner and numbly let herself be carried by the crowd. She found herself at the rifle range.

She'd never shot at anything before. But in her mind's eye it was Arabella, not the targets, that she saw — Arabella whom she couldn't get away from, no matter how she tried. She paid the last of her money and raised her gun. 'It would be lovely if you weren't there any more,' she said. BANG! BANG! 'Mum would have me instead. She doesn't want the two of us.' BANG! BANG! 'Dad can teach me about the farm and I can be their girl.' BANG! BANG! 'No one's ever given me a pet name. You don't know how I felt when she called you 'Belle . . . '

BANG! BANG!

She handed back the rifle and stood brushing bright tears out of her eyes. She walked away, not seeing where she went. All she knew was that the necklace had started stinging again and the air was full of something coming, coming . . . She turned a corner and found herself in front of a large, striped tent. A fluttering sign announced:

GRANDMOTHER MARVELL'S MAGIC MIRRORS

Come and see yourself as you've never seen yourself before

MIRROR SPECTACULAR

A woman lifted the loose cloth of the tent door and stepped out into the sunlight. Her hair was dyed. You could see the white bits at the roots, could see beneath the powder and the lipstick and the flashy jet earrings that she was old. Godda's necklace *jumped* on Bonnie's neck and bit so hard that she cried out. The woman raised her eyes and looked at her.

It was the look she remembered from the tickling dream when her grandmother had said she'd never let her go. The look she'd had on that last day when Bonnie had opened the new flat door, and there she'd been on the doorstep with her suitcase in poor Doreen's hand. It was gloating. Triumphant.

'Well, well, well,' she said. 'And how are you?' . . .

It was Grandbag.

16

She should have expected it. There was, after all, another, different Maybelle on Highholly Hill, another Michael and another of herself. Why not Grandbag too? Perhaps she *had* expected it. She remembered her dream, and it suddenly seemed so worthless, all the running away, and the struggling and the pain. You couldn't escape things, could you?

The woman looked past Bonnie and smiled a smile that Bonnie knew, and that never changed. 'Magic mirrors, my dear,' she said. 'Real magic that can change your life.'

Bonnie turned to see whom she was speaking to. It was Arabella. She was breathless. She'd just come flying round the corner and stopped. Jake stood close against her legs and his ears lay flat against his head. Arabella . . . It was not to Bonnie that the woman looked with quiet, triumphant satisfaction. Not to Bonnie that the eyes said, 'I'll never let you go . . . '

'I haven't any money left,' Arabella said. 'What about you, Bonnie?'

'A free go, then,' the woman said. 'You can't miss Grandmother Marvell's Mirror Spectacular. You'll never see magic mirrors again. You'll wonder for the rest of your life what they were like.'

Arabella stepped forward. She put her arm on Bonnie's.

'Come on. Let's. Even if they're not magic, it's a free go . . . '

The woman glanced at Bonnie, without interest.

'That's right,' she said. 'And your friend can come too, if she wants. You can both have a free go.'

Bonnie, stunned, felt distant pain around her neck. Through it, she thought, 'She doesn't recognize me. She wants Arabella. She came for me, I know she did. *I know she did*. But she's found Arabella instead. I'm safe.' And as if it were inevitable, as if she had no choice about it, she said in a voice that sounded oily and cunning and quite unlike her own, 'You go on in, Arabella. I'll just tie up Jake. We don't want him in the way.'

Grandmother Marvell lifted the tent flap, and Arabella stooped beneath her arm and disappeared. Jake suddenly came alive. He made to rush forward, but Bonnie caught him by his collar and dragged him back. He lashed at her, but determination made her deft. She dug string out of her pocket and tied him up. He howled.

From inside the tent, Arabella's voice called her. 'Bonnie, *Bonnie*, come and look at this!' Jake stopped lashing. He just looked at her, appealed with his eyes.

'You don't understand,' she said. 'You don't know what you're asking. I can't stop now. Stop looking like that. Oh, I hate you, Jake. I do.' She got up and started walking towards the tent.

'I'm coming,' she called, and Jake howled again and strained to get free.

Inside the tent, Bonnie gasped. A glittering world lay behind the drabness of the canvas. Hot lights twinkled above mirrors, creating an unexpected dappled brightness like sunlight on water. The mirrors lined the walls and reflected each other. She had the impression of standing in an oriental palace where doorway led into doorway, room led into room. Suddenly Arabella appeared.

'There you are.' said Bonnie. She stepped forward into a mirror and banged her nose. Arabella's voice, behind her, shrieked with laughter. A long row of repeating Arabellas laughed. She turned, and the real Arabella stood with her hand over her mouth and her eyes dancing.

'Isn't it lovely? It *does* look magical, doesn't it? It's the way she's placed the mirrors. Come over here. Come and look at yourself. Why's Jake howling like that?'

They stood in front of a mirror that made them tall like princesses, with long, long hair.

'He's just being bad,' Bonnie said. 'He wants to come in here but he can't. He might knock things over.'

'I don't like to hear him cry like that,' Arabella said. 'I'll go and tell him that we won't be long.'

'*You can't go yet.*'

They both jumped. Grandmother Marvell, tall as a giantess, stood behind them with her arms folded in front of her. They turned, relieved to find that in real life she was cut down to size.

'My dog's barking,' Arabella said. 'I ought to go and see what's wrong.'

'But you haven't seen the special room,' Grandmother Marvell said. 'I'll be gone when you come back. You won't have another chance.'

Arabella hesitated and Bonnie couldn't stop herself. The words came out in the wheedling tone that was not her own.

'He'll be all right just a minute longer. We don't want to miss anything.'

'That's right. And it won't take long,' Grandmother Marvell said. She lowered her voice, as if she didn't want even Bonnie to hear. 'I don't show everyone my special room. Not everyone appreciates the *real* magic of my show.'

Arabella blushed, curious and flattered. 'It really won't take long?'

'Just as long as you want,' the woman said. 'You'll soon be out again. And you needn't worry about your dog. I'll take care of him.'

'Quickly then,' Arabella said. The pitch of Jake's howls rose but she didn't seem to notice. 'I must admit, I can't bear the thought of missing anything. We'll see the special room.'

The woman led them in triumph down the tent, between the mirrors. She held up a flap at the end. Behind it, Bonnie could see a dark interior.

'Why does she want Arabella?' she thought. 'Why did Grandbag ever want me? Oh, nothing matters, does it? Nothing can change the way things are . . .'

Her feet stumbled forward. She followed Arabella, ducked under Grandmother Marvell's arm. She heard Jake's last shout.

'It's through the door at the end,' Grandmother Marvell said. She dropped the flap behind them, and there was silence. They were on their own, the two of them in the dark. What had she meant, the door at the end?

'Where are you, Bonnie? I can't see a thing.' Arabella bumped into Bonnie and grabbed her hand. 'It's funny in here. Can you see where we came in?'

'There's danger in here,' thought Bonnie. She could almost put out a hand and touch it. 'There's danger in here and Arabella won't ever come out again.'

'It smells funny,' Arabella said.

'It smells like darkness,' Bonnie thought.

'What's that?' Arabella said.

'Where?'

'Over there.'

Bonnie's eyes made out a distant, grey, light. 'I don't know,' she said. 'Let's find out, shall we? She said we had to look for a door.'

She stepped forward, taking Arabella firmly in her hand. Suddenly the necklace seemed to rise up all round her neck. For a minute she thought that it would strangle her. She felt hot pain. She felt it like a pair of angry hands.

She stopped. Gasped. Chewed into her lip to stop herself screaming. She tasted blood in her mouth.

'What is it?' Arabella said.

'It's . . . nothing.' Arabella couldn't see her face. She couldn't see the bright tears or the sweat. And what were the tears for? Were they just for the pain, or were they for her — because she couldn't stop now, she had to go on? *'Come on.'*

They edged their way towards the light. Bonnie's heart pounded. Her neck roared with pain. She didn't know how she kept herself from crying out, how she kept them moving forward. Hot rivers of sweat rolled down her face. If ever there was a moment when she should turn about, take Arabella away, surely this was it. And yet she didn't. She saw the outline of the door, flush with the wall and painted black so that you hardly knew it was there.

'We've found it,' she heard her voice say.

Arabella peered through the gloom, and the thundering pain round Bonnie's neck went away. Everything became quiet and still. She pinched her hand. She was real. She could think clearly again. Whatever happened next, she would have no excuses.

'You go first,' she said. She put her hand on the door and it swung open. She saw a huge, grand mirror in a gilt frame, glinting out at them like secret eyes beneath closed lashes. She stepped behind Arabella. Then, distantly, she heard an angry cry which reminded her of Grandbag. She heard something rushing towards them both . . .

'It's too late,' she thought with her new, dreadful clarity. 'Whatever it is, it's too late. Arabella's gone.'

But she was wrong. Something rushed beneath the tent flap, bringing momentary light with it. Arabella, on the threshold, hesitated. It rushed towards them and then past. It brushed their legs as it tumbled through the door.

It was Jake. Bonnie watched him go. He ran wildly, howling, into the mirror. She watched him go, go, go. She heard his scream becoming fainter, saw his body grow small, small, small. And then, in a split second, but as if it had taken minutes, he was gone, leaving behind him only the faint smell of, what was it, death . . . ?

Arabella screamed. Bonnie felt her hand go out and this was the dreadful thing she'd always known she could do. This was what she'd come here for. She knew, as she watched herself in fascinated, clear slow motion, that she was reaching for Arabella's back, that she was pushing her into the mirror after Jake, that she was going to get rid of her for ever. Her head was no longer full of the fuzz of pain that made everything unreal. This was really her, and she was really doing it.

Then her hand gripped Arabella by the shoulder. It pulled her back. Pulled her away. She heard a distant, unexpected voice, and it was her own voice, shouting, 'Come on, Arabella, come on, we've got to get away.'

They ran together down the dark room, bursting through into the blinding brightness of mirrors and lights. Grandmother Marvell crouched, reflected a hundred times on every side, nursing her hand where Jake had bitten it. They pushed a pathway through, out towards the long-forgotten world outside. Out into the showground.

Then they ran as neither of them had ever run before. Round the corner, past the rifle range, back towards the judging tent, round behind the pens, into the car park where they found the Land Rover and tumbled in among the safe smells and familiar sights and bits and pieces of home, Florence's jacket, Mum's bag, Dad's spare tobacco pouch . . .

'What happened, Bonnie?' Arabella asked, when she

17

They sat up in the back of the barn, high among the bales, with the soft material of the balloon tumbling between them onto the stone floor. Mice scuffled in a distant corner and farm cats prowled between lean shafts of sunlight, looking for the next meal.

Bonnie told it *all*: Maybelle and Michael and the midnight blue balloon and Grandbag. How she felt about Mum and Dad, about Highholly Hill. How she'd felt about Arabella, felt when Mum said ''Belle''. About the night she'd seen them all together in the bed, about the rifle range and the way she'd put her hand on Arabella's back to push her into that last mirror . . .

She couldn't stop it now. She couldn't spare herself, and now Arabella would hate her. She'd tell Mum and Dad and they'd hate her too. Her life upon the hill fell about her like a house of cards. This, not running away, was how it would end. She told about Wild Edric and the Lady Godda. She told about the necklace, unbuttoned her blouse to show it off. Arabella's drooping head looked up.

A shaft of teatime sunlight fell on the gold heart of the flower and the blue enamel. They shone with all the richness of autumn leaves and the brightness of a clear sky. There was more to this story than just hate. Arabella leaned across and touched the necklace lightly, nervously. Its diamonds glinted like rainbow tears.

'Now I know why you fumbled with your collar,' she said.

Bonnie nodded grimly and twisted it round. 'It's cooled down now,' she said. 'It doesn't burn any more.' She struggled with the silver hands again. 'I still can't get it off. You ought to have it. It's your hill, not mine.'

She tugged again and Arabella imagined Godda's necklace lost for ever in little bits, down, down, down among the straw. 'Be careful,' she said. 'You might break it.' She touched the thing again. Godda's necklace. She thought of the painting in Mum's sitting-room. Thought of the Throne on the top of the hill.

'They're *real*, aren't they?' she said.

'What?' said Bonnie.

'Wild Edric and the Lady Godda. They gave you the necklace and they saved us both. They did what Mum's stories say they do. They guarded their hill. Looked after us. They're really down there, somewhere.'

Bonnie remembered the shaking ground. She remembered how she'd tried to get off the hill and how she'd failed. They'd *made* her find that necklace, hadn't they, and she was the only one who'd have understood what it warned about. She was the only one who knew Grandbag . . .

'Yes,' she said. 'They must be real.'

They looked at each other. Out beyond the barn door, Dad whistled in the yard. There was no pattering of Jake's feet following him. No matter what had happened, what Bonnie had felt, no matter how things were between them still, it wasn't over yet.

'All she's got's a dog, and if she's really like Grandbag — and she surely is — she'll be *awful* because she hasn't got her way. You've no idea how mad she'll be. She's bound to try to get you again.'

'But why? There seems no reason.'

'If you knew Grandbag, you'd understand. She sees things, you see, and they have to be hers. She even takes things sometimes. It's awful. And it's not just things. It's people too. If someone's hers, she'll never let them go.

109

She wouldn't let me go. And in a funny sort of way she didn't give a chance to Maybelle either.'

'Perhaps she loved you both so much.'

'Oh no. It wasn't like that. She doesn't love anything. It's *greed*.' Bonnie's face was lined and tight and tired now. 'Maybe this new grandmother has seen the hill and wants it,' she said. 'Maybe it's you she wants. I don't know. But it won't stop there. Don't you see? She'll want Mum too, and Dad and Mr and Mrs Onions. Maybe even Edric and Godda. She'll want the house. She'll want the barns. She'll want the sheep and the cattle and the holly grove and the stones on the top. She'll want *everything* . . .'

Arabella shivered. 'What'll we do?'

Bonnie looked through the criss-cross shafts of sunlight, through the cracks in the door, up towards the house. There was only one thing to do, and then Mum and Dad would know all about her, know the horrid things she'd done.

'We'll have to tell them what happened,' she said, swallowing hard. 'We'll have to warn them.' She slid forward and scrambled from the bales. When she got to the ground she brushed herself down and stretched her stiff limbs. 'Will they believe us?'

'I don't think Dad will,' Arabella said, following her down. 'He doesn't dream of magic things. The holly grove, for instance. It's just a grazing site for him. A bit of pathway up the hill. Nothing strange at all. But Mum might. She belongs to to the hill, you see. It's where her family's always been. She was brought up with the idea of Wild Edric. She knows there are funny things about this hill.'

'Well, we'd better tell her then,' Bonnie said. 'Grandmother Marvell won't waste any time and neither should we.' She made for the door, anxious to get the awful moment over. Arabella watched her.

'You won't go, will you Bonnie?' she suddenly said.

Bonnie turned and stared in surprise.

'What was that?'

'When this is all over,' Arabella said, surprised at herself too. 'When Grandmother Marvell's gone and everything's safe again, you won't fly off and leave us, will you? You know . . . ' She held up the blue stuff of the balloon and managed a shaky smile, 'fly off in your balloon.'

Bonnie couldn't move. 'I *hated* you.'

'I know.'

'I could have killed you.'

'But you never did.'

Cats and mice scrambled. Sparrows chattered outside. Arabella was saying that, despite it all, things between them were all right. It couldn't have been easy and Bonnie thought, 'But I don't deserve to stay. It *isn't* all right. She might forgive me but I can't forgive myself.'

A voice broke into their thoughts. 'Arabella, Bonnie . . . ' It was Mum, up on the terrace.

Bonnie tugged the barn door. It shuddered open. 'We'll talk about it later,' she said. 'There are more important things to do.' And she walked away.

After tea, Mum went straight to bed. Her face was pale and strained and, despite her reluctance, Dad hurried her away.

'You never feel well after the Show,' he said. 'It's a lot of work for you, first the harvest and then preparing all those cakes and things. Come on, don't argue. I'll see to Florence, and the girls will clear up the tea.'

'I feel so silly,' said Mum. 'And I meant to go back down and look for Jake.'

'He'll look after himself,' Dad said. 'He's no fool, that dog. You couldn't really lose him. You wait and see, he'll be back again in the morning.'

It was Bonnie's chance, but Dad got hold of Mum and pushed her through the door and up the stairs. Bonnie began washing up plates, not knowing whether she was sorry or relieved. She wiped the wooden table and set Mum's prize-winning flower arrangement in the middle of it. She looked past it to the empty place beneath the window where Jake always lay. Perhaps she should have followed Mum upstairs . . .

She watched Arabella put Dad's trophy for the best milking cow up on the shelf next to the stove. She watched Dad disappear with Florence and her nightdress towards the bathroom. No matter what Arabella said, no matter whether she told Mum today or tomorrow, her days were numbered, weren't they?

'What'll we do now?' Arabella said, when Dad had gone. 'Should we go and see if Mum's awake and tell her?'

'I don't know,' Bonnie replied.

'Shall we leave it till the morning?'

'I don't know.'

'Will Grandmother Marvell come in the night?'

'I don't know what she'll do!'

'It's not like Mum to go to bed.' Arabella sighed. 'And you know, she usually notices, even when I don't say, if something's wrong.'

Dad reappeared. 'Florence fell asleep before I even got her into bed,' he said. 'Let's go and light a fire in the sewing-room. It's always the same after the Bank Holiday Show. There's that hint of something . . . autumn . . . in the air.'

'I'd like to go out,' Bonnie said. 'If that's all right. I'll join you later.'

'Of course,' said Dad. He filled his arms with kindling from the firebox, and newspaper and matches. 'But don't be long now. I haven't forgotten how early you started. You've had quite a day.'

It was a relief to stand out on the terrace in the clear, fresh air. Good to get out of the house and to be quiet and to hear the owls fluttering above the trees and to watch a harvest moon rising.

Bonnie slid through the gate into the orchard, up between the trees, over the stile, up the meadow. It was cool now, and getting dark. She reached the holly grove, stooped between low branches.

'Where are you?' she called. There was no reply. 'I know you're here,' she called again. 'Look, I need to talk . . .'

There was still no reply. She looked all around her. Nothing stirred. Not a shadow flickered. If she'd thought he'd know what she should do, if she'd thought he'd be a friend, she'd been a fool.

'Of course,' she whispered angrily. 'You're not a person. You don't care what happens. I forgot.'

She climbed back out of the grove. The farmhouse lay below her. Smoke was rising from the chimney and she thought of Dad and Arabella round the fire and Mum and Florence in bed. Then she saw the lights of the fairground brightening as the sky grew darker. She thought of Jake as she made her way back to the house.

18

Arabella woke up. She stumbled out of bed, heady with sleep, and fumbled her way, hardly knowing what she was doing, into her dressing-gown. In the back of her mind she knew it wasn't really morning, wasn't time to get up yet. But all the same, she made her way down the stairs. There was something, wasn't there, something that had woken her up, something she maybe had to do and didn't want to think about . . .

The kitchen was full of steely dawn. The first of the grey morning light caught the kettle by the side of the stove. Everything was still and quiet. Arabella stooped and opened the wheel that let the air into the stove. She lifted the big lid and set the kettle on the hob. The pipes began at once to hiss with the new day's life. What *was* it that she didn't want to think about? Oh, she couldn't get her head out of the clouds of sleep. She tightened the dressing-gown around her and fumbled with the latch. She tiptoed through the scullery and struggled with the bolts and crept outside.

The hilltop was clear, but the valley was smudged with thick, white mist, out of which only a church spire and the tallest trees protruded. Arabella sighed. Oh dear. She had no memories like trees to peep out of her sleepy mists. Why had she woken so early? What was she doing out here?

And then she called Jake. She didn't know what made her do it, because she wasn't dressed for a walk and her feet were cold and bare. But she called, 'Jake, Jake, come here boy . . . ' and he didn't come. And then she remembered.

It was as if she'd swallowed a lump of ice and it had got stuck halfway down. As if she were sinking like a bag of drowning kittens in a pond. She stared at the misty valley. Was there a showground down there? Were there marquees, the remains of yesterday's pens and stalls, a tent of magic mirrors? Perhaps she'd imagined it all. Perhaps it was all a dream . . . She called Jake again. Once more there was no reply. But he could be out on an early morning jaunt with Dad. They did go out early sometimes, didn't they? Go off shooting crows and pigeons?

The sun broke over the top of the hill. It would be hot later. It always was, after mornings like this. It shone on the hilltop, making it alive and shiny and green. It shone on the mist, which began to melt away. Arabella made out roofs and hints of hedgerows. She saw Hope Dingle. She made out flags and the top of a roundabout and the marquees . . .

There *had* been a Show. She hadn't dreamed it . . . There *had* been a tent of magic mirrors.

Back in the kitchen, the kettle bubbled cheerfully now. Jake's place by the window was bare. Leaving the boiling kettle to steam the windows, Arabella crept back wretchedly through the house and up the stairs. She found Bonnie lying in bed, fiddling miserably with Godda's necklace.

'There you are,' she said. 'I wondered where you'd gone. It's bothering me again. Is Mum awake yet?'

'It's not very likely. Do you know the time?'

Bonnie squinted at the clock. 'A quarter to six. Your feet are blue. What have you been doing?'

Arabella pulled off her dressing-gown. She didn't want to talk. She wanted to think. She got back into bed.

'What are you doing?'

115

'I'm cold. There's nothing we can do just yet. I'm going back to sleep.

She lay looking out of the window over her bed. Above the meadow, Edric's Throne was on fire with pink morning light. 'Even if we tell Mum,' she thought, 'we won't get Jake back.'

When Arabella awoke again, Florence was crawling across the floor.

'Hello, Florence,' she said. 'Come here. That's right. Come here, you clever girl.'

She sat up and pulled Florence onto the bed. Florence kissed her with her wet, red lips and put her soft head against her cheek. She thought of Grandmother Marvell getting her, thought of that last mirror, and held her hard. Bonnie was pulling back the curtains from the front window and looking out, pronouncing it the brightest and best of days. Arabella got up, Florence still in her arms, and peered over Bonnie's shoulder. The mist was all gone. The sun was bright and breakfast high. The morning birds were singing. But it was not, they both knew it, the brightest and best of days.

'Let's go and find Mum,' Arabella said, heavily.

'All right,' said Bonnie, with a sigh.

But the bedrooms were empty. Arabella frowned, surprised. There was no sign of Mum or Dad, and it was never quiet like this. You could always hear Mum singing, and the sound of laughter and voices downstairs.

'Something's not right.'

They tumbled downstairs, into the kitchen.

'*There* you are,' said Dad. 'And Florence. Give her to me. I was just coming to get you. Breakfast's ready. Sit down.'

The girls stared. Mum sat at the table, weakly stirring a cup of tea. Dad stood over the stove, with steam rising

116

from bacon and eggs and frying tomatoes. The kettle boiled. The toast popped. Mum didn't move.

'What's wrong, Mum?' Arabella said.

Mum looked up at her and smiled weakly. 'Nothing's wrong,' she said, and she reached out and touched her flower arrangement in the centre of the table. 'Which of you put it there? They look really nice, don't they? I'm tired, that's all. You may not have noticed it, but we've had a harvest these last couple of weeks, and yesterday we had the Show.'

'The grain man will be here in a minute,' Dad said. 'I'll have to go. Can you girls help me get this food on the table?'

They piled breakfast onto plates. Mum wrinkled her nose. 'Really,' she said. 'I couldn't. Not today.'

'I think you should,' Dad said.

She shrugged, reached for an orange from the bowl and began to peel it. 'This will do for me,' she said. 'Don't look like that. I'm quite all right. Give me half an hour to wake up. Bonnie, could you feed Florence for me?'

There was the sound of an engine chugging into the yard. Dad began to fling himself into his overalls. There was a scraping of the scullery door and footsteps out there and then the latch lifting on the kitchen door. Mr Onions' face appeared. 'Mr Evans is here,' he said.

'I'm just coming,' said Dad. 'Girls, you stay and help Mum.' He took a few quick mouthfuls of breakfast. 'You can come out when you've finished in here,' he said. 'But make sure you've finished. I don't want Mum left to do everything.'

He made for the door. Bonnie put Florence in her high chair.

'I'll ask if Mrs Onions can come down, shall I?' he said to Mum, who smiled thinly, and nodded. Then he was gone.

Bonnie fed Florence and finished her own breakfast. She watched Mum eat the orange and suck her fingers clean. She still wore her dressing-gown. And her hair, usually so carefully pinned and combed, hung over her shoulders in untidy tails. Maybelle's hair was always like that, and she always wore a dressing-gown at breakfast time, and she always slouched over the table as if she couldn't wake up, and sniffed at food and stirred and stirred her cup of tea . . .

Arabella glared at Bonnie. They were alone. Now was her chance. Why wasn't she saying anything? She took a deep, nervous breath. It had been almost easy, telling Arabella in the first relief of their escape. It had all just tumbled out. But this was different. She didn't know where to begin. Her mouth went dry. What should she say?

'Jake's not back,' Mum said, helpfully. 'I can't understand it. I thought he would have been by now. I'm feeling quite bad because I didn't go down again last night to look for him.'

'Jake isn't coming back.' Bonnie seized her chance. Her voice came out all harsh and lumpy. She hardly could believe that it was hers. 'We didn't just lose him, like we said. We didn't want to tell you. You see, something happened.'

Mum stared foggily at her. 'What do you mean?'

'It could happen to you all,' Bonnie went on. 'You, Florence, Dad, Arabella . . . '

Out in the yard, there was a sudden din of tractors turning and men shouting, engines revving, vehicles negotiating. Mum frowned. She got up and closed the window. 'Say that again . . . '

'Jake's not coming home,' Bonnie said. 'You see . . . ' Mum turned from the window with her puzzled frown. 'Jake's dead,' Bonnie said. 'We saw him die.'

The scullery door shuddered again, and there were footsteps.

'No,' said Mum. She shook her head. 'No, Bonnie, you've got that wrong.'

'She hasn't,' Arabella said. 'I saw it too.'

The latch lifted on the kitchen door, and it was opened. 'Is anybody home?'

Jake came bounding in.

19

Bonnie recognized the voice straight away. She could see the black-and-bead-coat in her mind's eye, seconds before the kitchen door opened properly and Grandmother Marvell appeared, wearing, as it turned out, not Grandbag's famous coat, but a searing green, gaudy, summer dress.

'Didn't mean to startle you,' she said, twitching at the neckline of the dress. 'Found him this morning underneath my trailer. Someone said he was yours. He *is* yours, isn't he? People get so attached to their animals, don't they?'

She stood, untypically hesitant, on the threshold. Her voice, Bonnie realized, was struggling to be soft and nice. She smiled round at them, even at Bonnie, whom yesterday she'd more or less ignored. If it hadn't been for the bandaged hand, where Jake had bitten it, Bonnie might have been confused. That, and the sudden stinging pain around her neck, and a quick dart of the eyes that took in everything, so that Bonnie could imagine her, just as Grandbag might have done, adding Dad's silver cup and Mum's flower arrangement and the hanging lamp and the old copper pans to some nasty, greedy jackdaw's hoard somewhere.

Jake sniffed his way round the room. He stopped at Mum's feet. Mum ruffled his hair. Her tired face smiled over his head at the visitor.

'Yes, he's our dog. How kind of you to bring him home. Come in and sit down. Come on. Don't just stand there. We *were* getting a bit worried because he never usually runs away.'

'You're busy,' Grandmother Marvell said. 'There's all that going on outside and you haven't even finished breakfast. It's not a time to call, I know. I'm sure you've got lots to do, and I don't want to hold you up. What a *lovely* baby you have. How old is she? What a lovely house this is.'

'We're not busy,' Mum said. 'Of course you're not holding us up. I'll put the kettle on. It's the least I can do after you've come up here, all this way. It is a nice house, isn't it?'

Grandmother Marvell allowed herself to be persuaded in. She sat down at the table and looked around. Her cold eyes throbbed with good will but there was something behind that good will, wasn't there?

'We don't often get visitors,' Mum said. 'The track, you know. Did you come up with the grain man?'

'I brought my car,' Grandmother Marvell said. 'It wasn't too difficult.'

Bonnie stared out of the window at an ancient car. It was just Grandbag's sort of thing. She remembered a succession of rusty Cortinas and a creaking Hillman that smoked on every hill. She stared beyond the car, at the twisty track and the distant valley. How had Grandmother Marvell got the thing up here? And there was a huge, wrapped bundle tied onto the roof-rack. It must have been impossible trying to shift that lot up the bumpy track, especially over the little bridge and between the deep ruts of the twisty canyon.

What *was* that bundle on the roof-rack?

Arabella was sitting at the table now and Mum was telling Grandmother Marvell their names. She poured boiling water into the teapot. The surprise of a visitor had stripped her of her sleepiness. She looked like herself again. That was more than Bonnie could say for Jake. He stood awkwardly on the rug by the stove as if he didn't know what to do, or where to go. He looked so *lost* . . .

'He's not himself,' said Mum.

'Poor thing,' said Grandmother Marvell. 'He missed you all. He was really unhappy. That's why I thought I'd better bring him back as quick as possible.'

'He's feeling ashamed,' said Mum. 'That's what's wrong with him. He's never gone off like that before.' She looked across at Bonnie. 'He loves going out with you,' she said. 'Why don't you take him for a run, Bonnie? Let him stretch his legs and feel at home again.'

'But . . . ' Bonnie began.

'Arabella, get the teacups will you?' Mum went on. 'Bonnie, we'll save you a cup. You don't have to take him on a real walk or anything. Just let him run up and down.'

Bonnie hovered. How could she go? What would happen when her back was turned? What would Grandmother Marvell do? Her eyes met Arabella's. 'I don't know what to do,' they said, and Arabella's eyes said the same.

'Go on,' said Mum. 'Or the tea will get cold.'

Out on the terrace, Jake began to sniff and explore. Bonnie followed him away from the busy yard, up into the orchard. She talked to herself. 'I don't understand it,' she said. 'We saw him die. We did . . . '

The necklace stung her again.

'Oh, wretched, wretched necklace,' she said. 'Why can't you tell me what'll happen next? Why can't you tell me what to *do*?'

She sat on the edge of the well, where she could see up between the trees, towards Edric's Throne. 'If you're really there, why can't you come and help us? A stupid, stinging necklace is *useless* on its own. We want to see you with your horses and flowing hair and jewels . . . '

Her eyes turned back to Jake. He was standing very still. He didn't seem to look at anything. He didn't, somehow, seem like Jake.

'Jake,' Bonnie called. 'Jake, come here!'

He came up to her, but not as though in answer to her call. His response seemed detached, almost accidental. He lifted his head and stared at her. It was as though he'd never seen her before. As if he was a stranger.

'What's the matter with you?' Bonnie said, and as she said it she knew. As she put out her hand and felt the dog that looked like Jake, she knew he wasn't. He didn't feel the same. He didn't smell the same or behave the same. He only looked the same. And, when you lifted his face and looked into those pale, limp eyes, he didn't even really *look* the same. Bonnie let the dog go. Relieved that the scrutiny was over, he turned away and began his half-hearted explorations again.

'You're not Jake.'

At that moment, Dad turned the tractor in the yard. She looked up at the noise, and caught a brief glimpse of him between the trees. 'Would he know,' she said to herself, 'if Mum and Arabella disappeared and Grandmother Marvell sent back empty shells instead?'

'Of course he would,' she said right back. And then, 'No, he wouldn't. Oh, he'd know *something* was wrong. But he'd never think, nobody would, that they were really *gone*.'

She got up and began to run back towards the house. So where was Jake really? What had Grandmother Marvell done with him? If she captured Mum and Arabella and Florence, where would they all go? Would they be dead? Would they be in some dark, bodiless, terrible place, never to be set free again?

'No one would ever come and rescue them. No one would know. It would be worse than death, and all the time there'd be . . . ' she looked towards the Jake-creature, 'things like that, here in their place. And no one would know.'

She squeezed frantically through the orchard gate and ran along the terrace, through the scraping scullery door, through the musty darkness, back, with pounding heart, into the kitchen.

Mum sat at the table, with her tea. Arabella leaned over her. Grandmother Marvell was laughing the ordinary, friendly laugh of one who enjoys good company and has not a bad thought in the world. Postcards were spread in front of them. They were all looking and laughing and turning them over. It was a happy scene. Grandmother Marvell's jet-shiny hair bounced as she laughed, her red lips parted. She smoothed down her dress. But as Bonnie got close she saw that the hair was dyed, the smooth face was powdered thickly, the skin beneath the lipstick was wrinkled and coarse. That things were not what they seemed to be.

She too peered over Mum's shoulder. The postcards were of exotic places. Arabella, by her side, hardly seemed to notice that she was back, but Grandmother Marvell looked up and wrapped her long fingers round her cup of tea and said in a voice that had an edge to it, 'How's that dog, then? Settled down, has he?'

Bonnie looked at the stringy fingers. the long, painted nails. The fingers were just like the ones in the tickling dream. Grandmother Marvell's nails clacked against the china cup. Clack, click! She smiled at Bonnie, and Bonnie remembered how Grandbag loved to taunt. She remembered those nails digging into her and she thought, 'Maybe it was a dream, but once it was something more, wasn't it? It used really to happen.'

Clack, click!

Arabella turned a flushed, unnatural, excited face, a face that made Bonnie feel cold inside, towards Grandmother Marvell. It was as if she'd been bewitched. As if she'd forgotten yesterday. She brandished a card.

'Have you really, *really* been there?' she said.

'Of course I have,' Grandmother Marvell replied. She took the card and looked at it. 'I've been everywhere.'

'I've never been anywhere.'

Grandmother Marvell smiled, as if this was what she'd waited for. 'In that case, there's something outside that I'd like you to see,' she said. She looked at Mum, and so did Bonnie. Mum was flushed too. What had she done to them both? 'I wonder if that nice husband of yours would help me get it down. Then we can unwrap it.'

'Oh,' said Mum, 'what is it?'

'You'll see,' said Grandmother Marvell. 'You'll never have a chance like this again. Come on.'

Bonnie knew now, even without Godda's necklace leaping warnings round her neck, what was wrapped and tied to the top of the car. It was the magic mirror, wasn't it? She looked desperately to Arabella, but Arabella was rising as if she had no choice. She wouldn't meet Bonnie's eyes.

'Mum . . . ' Bonnie said.

'What is it, Bonnie?'

'Don't go, Mum. Don't go out there.'

Mum hesitated. Grandmother Marvell leaned across the table and focused on Mum's eyes. She spoke very softly, as if it was just between the two of them. 'You'd like to know the future, wouldn't you?' she said. 'Don't say a thing. I *know*. You've got things on your mind. I saw right away when I walked in, that there are things you'd like to know.'

Mum's face flushed up bright, like Arabella's. It was as if Grandmother Marvell had tapped some spring of secret things inside her. 'You can't *really* tell the future,' she said lightly, dismissingly. But her voice, in between the words, said, 'Please, please do.'

Grandmother Marvell tapped her nails together and smiled her best smile. Mum got up to go.

'WAIT!' Bonnie shouted.

They all stared. What could she do? 'I . . . I want to come too. Will you just wait for me? Will you just wait a minute?'

For the first time Grandmother Marvell's eyes lost

125

their battle to be nice. They became Grandbag's angry black eyes and Bonnie thought, 'If I beat her now, I'm beating Grandbag too. If I can get rid of her, I'm getting rid of Grandbag. Whatever do I mean by that? I don't know. What am I going to do? I *don't know* . . . !'

'Of course we'll wait,' said Mum. 'I'll wash up the cups. We'll all go out together.'

'I won't be long.'

Bonnie raced up the stairs. She could halt the process for a minute, but she'd have to come back down again, and what would happen then? She climbed the attic stairs too. She hadn't been up there since the first day, hadn't even thought of it, but the stinging necklace seemed to drive her on. It weighed a ton and was hot like fire. Oh, Edric and Godda! She slid through the hatch, clambered along the attic, peered out of the window at the end. There was no Edric on horseback, waiting between the apple trees to rescue them. No Godda. Was this the best they could do?

'Edric, Godda, help me please. At least give me an idea . . .'

She opened the skylight, slid out onto the roof and down onto the flat bit. Looking over the little wall she saw that the Bank Holiday Show, down in the valley, was being dismantled. Marquees were collapsing, rides were being taken down, lorries were driving across the showground onto the road. Oh, it was a long, long way down there, and yet something from it had struggled all that way up the hill to get them. It was here, in the yard, tied to the top of an old car. She looked down. It was a long way to the ground. Oh, where were Edric and Godda?

A long way to the ground . . .

Bonnie's heart fluttered. She swallowed hard. She looked. A long way to the ground . . . If she fell, she'd break her back or her leg, or her head would split open and she'd bleed all over the place. If she fell, they'd have

126

to rush her off the hill to hospital. They wouldn't have time for unwrapping magic mirrors.

It was just like being in the tent again. Like when she put out her hand to push Arabella into the mirror and her arm had gone ahead of her and she felt detached from things. Everything went slow. She climbed onto the little wall, watched herself. Slithered along the edge.

She watched her body go. No hand this time reached out to grab her back. Then the film changed speed. The terrace rushed at her. She never knew before that when you fell, you did it so fast . . .

20

There was a thud outside. It wasn't like the sounds out there already, the reverberating tractor engine or the clatter of the gate or grain tumbling into Evans' truck, with its succession of small sucks and echoes. It was softer than these sounds and yet they all heard it, muffled, unresounding, flat and sore as a bruise.

Mum looked up sharply. The flushed look disappeared from her face. Arabella shook her head as if a spell had been broken. Outside, someone switched off the tractor engine.

'What was that?' said Mum, as if she knew it was something dreadful.

There were shouts in the yard, and footsteps coming up onto the terrace. Dad rushed past the kitchen window, followed by the grain man and Mr Onions and Henry and Ned. Mum dropped everything and made straight for the door. Arabella followed her. They stumbled through the darkness of the scullery, tripping over each other in their eagerness to get outside. Mum hauled back the scullery door. Arabella chased her down the step. The crowd of men at the end of the terrace looked up at the sight of them. What was it, down there between them? They shifted slightly, and Mum and Arabella saw.

There, on the ground between the men, lay Bonnie. Her eyes were closed. Her body was strewn across the stones like an unloved rag doll that had been thrown away. Her hair was spread around her and her head lay right beside a great stone flower trough. Another inch, and it would have been split open.

Mum pushed between them all. Arabella did the same. Bonnie's face was parchment white. There was not a movement, not even a breath. Arabella remembered that first morning, when Bonnie had been a stranger lying exhausted and weak and dew-drenched in the holly grove. This time it was different. Bonnie wasn't a stranger any more. This time it was different. She was really dead.

'Mum,' she said. 'Oh, Mum . . . !'

Mum leaned forward. Dad got hold of Arabella by the shoulders and held her tight. Mum began to scrape Bonnie up into her arms. Her face too was ghastly white. She touched the necklace and looked up questioningly, towards the open attic window. Then she looked down again into Bonnie's face.

'Help me,' she said to the men. 'She's not dead. Help me get her indoors.'

Dad put Arabella aside. He reached down and, with gentle hands, took Bonnie from Mum. Mum stood aside and let him carry her back along the terrace.

They reached the scullery door, in a little procession. And Grandmother Marvell greeted them. She came out of the darkness as a farm rat comes from its lair. All the niceness was stripped away and the bright light of day was cruel to the face beneath the powdery make-up. Her eyes swept impatiently over the men and the bundle of Bonnie. As Mum and Arabella made to pass her by and follow the others, she plucked at Mum's arm.

'Leave it to the men,' she said, in a wheedling voice. 'Don't fret. They'll take her in, they'll sort her out, they don't need you, she'll be all right.' She plucked again. 'Come and see my mirror. You mightn't have another chance. Come on, do . . . '

Mum stared at Grandmother Marvell. Really stared at

129

her. As if she'd never seen her before. As if she recognized her for what she was even if she didn't know the *half* of what she was.

'Get off me,' she said, and she pulled her arm away. 'What's wrong with you? Can't you see what's happened?'

'But this matters more.' Grandmother Marvell said, as if she truly couldn't see what had happened. She smiled blindly, awfully, from one to the other of them, and there was no kindness in her voice now. 'You don't understand. This matters more.'

'It *doesn't* matter more,' Mum said, in a voice that anyone who knew her would never have argued with. 'It doesn't matter at all. Get away.'

There was a flicker of a pause while Grandmother Marvell registered surprise, rejection, failure. Then the smile disappeared like sunshine behind dark clouds. The black eyes shone like headlamps in a storm. The hand reached out again. Arabella recoiled. The hand was reaching for *her*. What was it about those fingers?

'You'd better come with me instead,' she said, fixing Arabella with her eyes. 'They don't need you in there. Come on. My magic mirror . . . '

Mum pushed Arabella ahead of her into the scullery and slammed the door behind her. She locked and bolted it. Locked the door, with someone on the step outside. What was she doing? This wasn't like her! She picked at her arm where Grandmother Marvell had touched her, as if she were trying to pluck even the memory of the touch away. Her hand shook. She looked up at the shut bolts.

'I've locked her out, 'Belle,' she said. '*I've locked her out.*'

A furious knocking began outside. Mum felt as if she could almost see those burning headlamp eyes through the thickness of the wood. She could almost see the knuckles hammering.

'We'll go inside and see how Bonnie is,' she said firmly.

Arabella looked uncertainly at the door. The bolts were shaking.

'She can't get in,' said Mum. 'Hundreds of years of storms have never knocked that door down. The best thing to do is to forget she's there.'

'But . . . '

'Forget she's there, Arabella, and she'll have to go away.'

Mum turned her back on the door, and led Arabella away.

Bonnie was laid out on the settee in the cold and unused living-room.

'Michael,' Mum said to Dad, 'why don't you open out the sofa bed in the sewing-room. It's much nicer in there. And Arabella, go and get some sheets . . . '

Mum sat with Bonnie while they were gone. She didn't even notice that the knocking had stopped now. The men hovered anxiously by the fireplace. Mr Onions said he'd go for his wife right away. Mum nodded and said thank you, and he went. Mum's shoulders sank. She looked drained and tired again. Bonnie's eyes flickered and she moaned slightly, and Mum leaned forward and felt her for broken bones. She heard the side gate creak and footsteps fade away. Then she heard the shaky old car turning, screeching in the yard, and clattering off.

'Who was she?' Dad said, coming back into the room.

'She doesn't matter. She's gone. She won't be back.'

'Should we go for the doctor?'

Mum looked down at Bonnie. 'Well, she's waking up,' she said, touching her cheek. 'Her bones don't seem to be broken, though goodness knows how. I think she'll be all right.'

'The bed's ready next door.'

'Let's take her through, then.'

When Bonnie came round, the first thing she saw was Mum's sewing-machine with its mother-of-pearl butterflies. Then she saw Edric and Godda looking down at her. They'd caught her as she fell, hadn't they, saved her — and they were still here. She looked up and tried to thank them. Godda's necklace shone down at her from round Godda's neck, and her hand was outstretched. Edric, with one hand upon his lady, smiled . . .

Then Bonnie saw the cracks in the paintwork across Edric's face, and the gilt frame. She realized she was in the sewing-room on the sofa bed. She was looking at the painting over the fire. Edric and Godda weren't really there.

And yet she had a memory of the earth coming up at her and their hands as light as angels' wings, as they brought her down. She closed her eyes and lived it again. The open attic window. The slide down to the flat bit and the wall. The hardness of that little wall. The almost-taste of her heart beating in her mouth as she pushed the bricks and mortar away. Then Edric and Godda and their hands. Then the darkness. She went through it again. And then again . . .

Somewhere close, someone was crying. She opened her eyes. Arabella was by her side. She felt something gently moving. It was Arabella's thumb rubbing the back of her hand. She turned her head and Arabella looked at her and wiped her eyes and smiled. She tried to speak to her, but she couldn't. Why was Arabella crying? What had happened? Oh, she had this memory of falling. But that was all she had. No memory of anything before. No understanding. What she wanted was peace, to go to sleep again, but how could she when she didn't know what had happened? She tried to speak again.

'She's gone,' Arabella whispered. 'She's gone away. It's all right now. Oh, Bonnie, she'd have got us both if it wasn't for you. I'd *never* have had the courage. You were so brave. I never would have *dared* to do what you did.

But it worked. Oh, Bonnie, Mum hated her. She showed herself for what she really was and she's gone and Mum'll never let her back.'

Bonnie frowned. She didn't understand. She didn't know what Arabella was talking about. And the fall recurred. Every time she blinked, every time she closed her eyes . . .

The door opened. Mum came in. 'Ah, you're awake,' she said and she smiled with relief. She sat down on Bonnie's other side. Bonnie struggled to speak to her as well.

'Don't,' said Mum. 'Not yet. There's plenty of time later. You fell out of the window but we think you're all right.' She smiled again and patted Bonnie on the arm and Bonnie looked up into Mum's eyes, with the shadows underneath them. 'Your bones don't seem to be broken,' she was saying. 'They should be, you know. You've been very lucky and you've got to rest.'

'I . . . I can't . . . remember . . . '

'You won't yet. Don't worry. You knocked yourself out,' Mum said. 'You're going to feel a bit confused, but it'll all come back when it's ready. You'll be all right . . . '

Bonnie fell asleep again and dreamed. She woke and slept and woke and slept again. Distantly, she became aware of Mrs Onions and Mum and Arabella. Then she came round and Dad was leaning against the fireplace, just looking and looking at her.

'This has all happened before, hasn't it?' she thought and a picture of herself in the bed upstairs crept timidly out of her mind. Then a picture of Mum sitting by the window, looking for all the world like Maybelle, and then another of Arabella standing in the doorway, looking just like her.

Then she began to remember other bits and pieces too. Pictures of the house, the yard, the orchard, the meadow, the dusty attic with its telescope and wooden beads and books in trunks, Dad standing in the dark with his pipe and his eyes glinting as he looked down the valley. Looked down the valley at what . . . ?

Something was missing, wasn't it? Something important. She looked around. Dad was gone. Arabella sat in the armchair by the fireplace. And suddenly the memory of Grandbag's face slithered out of her mind. She heard her emphatic voice say, 'Well, well, well, and how are you?' She saw her lift the tent flap and step outside, raise her eyes and look her special, gloating, triumphant look. Of course! She sat up. She cried out. Arabella came at once to her side.

'Bonnie,' she said, 'what is it?'

'Grandbag . . . ' Bonnie said.

'I told you,' Arabella said. 'Don't you remember? She's gone.'

Bonnie stared at her. Grandmother Marvell and Grandbag flickered in green-summer, black-bead pictures through her brain. Grandmother Marvell, Grandbag, Grandmother Marvell, Grandbag, Grandbag . . . Unwelcome memories rushed forth demented from her brain. So many things that wouldn't go away, even if the women themselves were gone. All the memories that were her life, tumbling forth like circus acrobats before her eyes. She couldn't see Edric and Godda shining above the fireplace any more. She couldn't see Arabella. And it didn't matter that they'd gone. For it didn't make any difference. The hot balloon of hatred hovered above her head, drank the smoke of her pain. Hatred of life, of people, of everything.

'Things can seem so pretty, so nice,' she found herself shouting at the mellow, soft room. 'But there's nothing you can really *trust*.'

It was like her real voice speaking for the first time, something deep inside herself daring to come out and make itself known. She closed her eyes again, tight, and held her hands together over them as if she were in pain.

Then Arabella's voice cut softly through her darkness, swelled with unexpected confidence.

'You're wrong, you know,' she said, leaning forward urgently. 'It doesn't have to be the way it was for you. Grandbag treating you the way she did, I mean. Not everyone's like her.'

Bonnie heard the new tone in the voice. Her hands didn't move. 'What do you mean?'

'Mrs Onions looked after me, you know, when Mum was expecting Florence,' Arabella said. 'She did it for ages. Mum was ill, you see, and we thought Florence might never get born. When Florence *was* born, she told me she'd love to have a baby too, and I said, "Why don't you?" And she laughed and said, "Some things aren't meant to be. I'm too old now."'

'I don't see what you're getting at,' Bonnie said, although she did.

'If anyone could have got greedy and nasty, you'd have thought it would have been her,' Arabella said. 'But she never did.'

The words dropped into the darkness in Bonnie's head. A picture began to form, of Mrs Onions with Florence nestled in her arms, making for the tea tent down at the Show. Mrs Onions, with her baby birds and sick badgers, and now Arabella too . . .

'You can trust her,' Arabella said. 'You can trust Mum. You can trust Dad. You can trust me . . . '

The door opened. It was Mum again, with a drink of some kind in her hand. 'Off you go, Arabella. I'll sit with Bonnie now.'

Arabella left, and Mum sat down and offered the drink. Bonnie's head spun. She wanted peace. *She wanted peace.* She didn't want the drink, or Arabella telling her she could trust people. And there was still something . . . some memory that clutched at her mind to get free . . . something that had not returned to her yet. What was it?

'Come on, Bonnie. Have this little drink. Open your eyes. Take your hands away. Don't leave us,' Mum said.

And it came to her. Just a little thing. She remembered Arabella out in the barn. 'Don't leave us, Bonnie,' she'd said. 'When it's all over, don't, you know, fly off with your balloon . . . '

'She may forgive me, but I'll never forgive myself. *I'll have to go.*'

That's what she'd said.

'What's the matter?' Mum said.

Tears began to splash down Bonnie's cheeks. She thought of Mrs Onions with somebody else's Florence in her arms. 'Life's not fair,' she said, and then, 'Oh please, oh please, I don't want to go . . . '

Mum put her arms around her and held her tight. She didn't say 'don't cry'. 'You don't ever have to go,' she said instead.

'Don't *ever* have to go?'

'We love you, Bonnie, you silly girl.'

'But you don't know what I've done. You don't know what really happened.'

'I don't want to know. It's over now. She's gone,' said Mum, as if she understood. And, as she said it, the strangest thing happened. The memories seemed to fade, slide, slither away as if they weren't real any more, as if they didn't matter.

'They've both gone,' thought Bonnie, though she didn't quite know why. '*Grandbag too . . .* '

PART SIX

The Magic Mirror

21

They sat in the meadow, eating blackberries and looking down on the farmhouse roof. Smoke from the kitchen chimney rose, straight and thin, into a morning sky. Bonnie tilted her head and followed its path up, up, up . . .

'I haven't looked at the sky for ages,' she said. 'Not the way I used to do. Funny how things change.'

Arabella looked all around her. 'It is, isn't it?' she said. 'I used to be so lonely and bored. Even when Florence came along. I can't imagine life without you now.'

'It's only a month since the Bank Holiday Show,' Bonnie said. She looked beyond the farmhouse roof, at the showground which had become a farmer's field again. 'It seems so long ago.'

'The leaves aren't yellow yet,' Arabella said. 'But things feel different.'

'Funny how things change.'

Mum came up through the orchard towards them. She leaned on the stile, Florence in her arms, and called.

'Bonnie, Arabella!'

She wore a thick cardigan over her frock and Florence wore a coat. The morning air was more than fresh. It was sharp. Things *were* changing. Arabella got up, brushing blackberry crumbs out of her lap. 'She'll want us to help,' she said. 'There'll be lots to do, with harvest supper tonight.'

They ran down the meadow and climbed over the

stile into the orchard, heavy now with apples and plums. Mum had set Florence down to crawl through the grass. She'd seated herself on the low wall of the blocked-up well and, as they approached, she patted the stones by her side.

'Sit down,' she said. 'There's lots to do today. Mrs Onions will be down soon to help me cook but, before she comes, I wanted to talk to you.'

There was something in her voice.

'It's school,' Arabella hissed. 'She's going to start school again. I thought we wouldn't get away with it much longer.'

They sat down. Florence crawled to them and pulled herself up.

'There's no simple way to tell you this,' Mum said. 'Dad wanted me to make an announcement at breakfast time, but I'm not much good at things like that. I'd much rather just slip it out while we're piling logs or picking plums or getting ready for the harvest supper. But, even then, it doesn't come out easily . . . '

She clasped and unclasped her hands. This *wasn't* about school.

'You must have noticed I haven't been quite right,' she said. 'It's a bit like last time. Doctor says I've got to be very quiet, and I might have to spend a lot of time in bed. I hope he's wrong, because I hate it. I'm not used to being ill and I get so cross with myself. It's going to be hard for you, Arabella. You've already put up with it once. I'm having another baby.'

Another baby? The girls sat, stunned. Then Florence stood all on her own, announcing in the only way she yet knew how, that *she* wasn't a baby any more. *Another baby*!

Bonnie fell upon Mum. She'd never thought she'd be part of a family where the Mum had a baby. 'Mum, oh Mum . . . Another baby? That's just *wonderful* . . . ' Her eyes shone with excitement and Mum caught hold of her and wobbling Florence too, and looked over their heads at Arabella.

'When, Mum?' was all Arabella said, quietly.

'March, April . . . If all goes well, of course.'

'You mean . . .'

'I mean we've got to be careful. We nearly lost Florence. We don't want to lose this baby.'

'But we won't,' Bonnie said. 'Of course we won't. There's two of us to help you this time. You won't have to worry about a thing. We can cook and clean and help with Florence, and Mrs Onions will help too.'

'I *am* pleased, Mum,' Arabella said. 'It's just . . .'

'I know,' said Mum. 'It was hard with Florence. Who'd have thought it would happen again. And so soon.'

'Are *you* pleased, Mum?' Arabella said.

'Yes, I am,' said Mum.

'And Dad?'

'He's delighted.'

Arabella's face broke into a smile and suddenly she was in Mum's arms too and all four of them were hugging each other and clinging on tight.

'You shouldn't teach us any more,' Arabella said. 'It'll make you too tired. And we won't have time for lessons anyhow. We'll be too busy helping.'

Mum laughed. 'You're an opportunist,' she said. 'Do you know what that means? You can look it up in the dictionary when we go in. It can be your first task. *Of course* I'm not letting you off school. It's important and you've got to do it. You'll understand how much it matters some day.'

'I hope it's a boy, this time,' Arabella said.

'I think I do too,' said Mum.

They sat very quietly. The sun rose in the sky. Mosquitoes hovered over the well. An apple fell off a tree, thudded in the long grass. Florence began to crawl again.

'Every life changes the world,' Mum said suddenly. 'It's frightening, really. It makes you cling to what you've got. It makes you fear the future.'

'That doesn't sound like you, Mum,' Arabella said.

Mum stretched and smiled and got up. 'Oh, I'm not so different from you. Impatient for change, yet anxious when I see it coming. Sometimes I want to make time stand still. Sometimes I can't *wait* for tomorrow to happen. Funny, isn't it?' She picked up Florence. 'Let's go and get that harvest supper ready.'

When they got back indoors, Dad had the trestle tables, down from the attic, in pieces all over the living-room floor.

'It's the same every year,' Mum said. 'Dad can't remember how to put the bits together, and I can't believe how dusty the place has got.'

She disappeared and returned with a vacuum cleaner, then mops and buckets and pots of polish and feather dusters. 'It always gets like this,' she said to Bonnie. 'It's because we hardly ever come in here in the summer months. It's a great room for the winter, though. We always have the Christmas tree in here. And it's certainly the only bit of the house that's big enough for a supper like this.'

'Who's coming?' Bonnie asked. The first trestle table was up. It looked very big and there were two more to come. Dad had gone back into the attic to find the missing bits.

'Oh,' said Mum, 'there'll be Henry and Ned and Evans and Mrs Evans, and the other people from behind Roundhill and Mr and Mrs Onions, of course . . . Has either of you seen Mrs Onions? Dad said she'd be down first thing. I haven't seen her for days.'

The girls shook their heads. They stood on either side of Mum's dilapidated vacuum cleaner, surveying the size of the task in hand. Bonnie clutched a feather duster.

Arabella valiantly said, 'We can do all this. You ought to rest.'

Mum smiled. She had a feeling it was the first of many times she'd hear those words. 'That's very kind of you,' she said. 'I'm going to take you up on that. But there's a lot of cooking I ought to do before I rest.'

Distantly, they heard the kitchen door scrape open, and a voice call. It was Mrs Onions.

'Good,' said Mum. 'Now I *can* get on. We're in here,' she called.

Mrs Onions' footsteps rang on the kitchen floor. Her face peered round the door. She looked hot and awkward.

'I meant to get down earlier,' she said. 'I meant to get down yesterday as well. I'm really sorry.'

'That's all right,' said Mum. 'Don't worry.'

'I . . . I want you to meet someone,' Mrs Onions said. 'I've got him out in the kitchen. He'll be very helpful. You could do with another pair of hands. He'll get those tables scrubbed in no time.'

Mum stared curiously. There was something odd about Mrs Onions this morning. Mrs Onions turned her head and called.

'Jim!'

Bonnie, not knowing why, slid secretively into the shadows of the inglenook. As she did so, a boy appeared. He sidled round the doorway, into the room. Mrs Onions hovered around him, proudly, nervously. He wore grey trousers and what must have been one of Mr Onions' checked working shirts which had been cut down. He had shiny, brown, untidy hair and rosy cheeks and bright brown eyes. He looked wild and strong and shy, like Mrs Onions' badgers and rabbits and wounded birds. His gaze passed by Bonnie in the shadows.

'I've found a *boy*,' Mrs Onions said. 'He hadn't got anywhere else to go, so he's staying with Mr Onions and me. If you like, he'll help to get the trestle tables sorted out. He could do all sorts of things. He's really quick and strong. I've never seen anything like it. He didn't even have a name, you know. We called him Jim, after Mr Onions' father.'

Mum smiled a welcome. She crossed the room and took the boy's hand. The boy tried a shaky smile back. He didn't speak.

'What a crowd we're becoming up here. What a day for surprises,' Mum said. 'You couldn't find a better place to stay than with Mrs Onions, Jim. I'm sure you'll be very happy there. Now if you really *would* be prepared to help us . . .'

She went on to talk about trestle tables. Arabella was sent away and brought back a bowl of soapy water. Mrs Onions said she'd get on with the pies and Arabella could help her. The boy seemed to relax.

'What world is this,' thought Bonnie — and, for the first time in a long while, she fingered Godda's necklace, which still hung round her neck — 'where children like us can be plucked off the hill and no questions are asked?'

'We'll be in the kitchen if you want us,' Mum was saying. She led Arabella away. She said something to Bonnie about beeswaxing trestle tables when they were dry. Then she was gone, leaving behind her the distant echoes of other words: 'This isn't like anywhere else you've been. It doesn't matter where you come from. We don't ask questions here.'

Bonnie came out of the darkness with her feather duster still in her hands. She stared at the boy. His skin was bright now. He seemed all muscles and flesh. Real blood surely ran through his veins. He looked so different.

'I've never cleaned a room before,' he said. 'You'll have to tell me what to do.'

He was, of course, the shadowboy.

22

She took him in, from head to foot. 'You've changed so much,' she said. 'I hardly recognize you.'

He looked down at his own hands, with their lifelines and branching blue and pink veins. 'I hardly recognize myself . . .'

'I came looking for you,' she said. 'I came up to the holly grove. You must have heard me call. I swore I'd never look for you again. I'd never talk to you again. I wanted a friend and you wouldn't answer me . . .'

Her voice shook. She was surprised at herself. Was it anger? Or was it the unexpectedness of it all?

He sighed. 'It seems so long ago now,' he said. 'You went away. I was so lonely. I did want to be friends, but the wanting frightened me. I'd never felt anything like that before, you see. The hill seemed cold and empty and hard after you had gone. And I was frightened. I could feel things in me changing. *changing*! I didn't feel like the same boy any more and I couldn't stop it . . .'

'It sounds like being born,' Bonnie said. She thought of Mum and the secret, dark, hidden baby she was having, locked away in a world just like his had been. No choices, no understanding who he was or where he was or where he came from or why he did the things he did . . . 'It sounds like growing up as well. Don't ask me what I mean. I don't really know, but Maybelle says it's terrible. How did Mrs Onions find you?'

His face lit up like a real boy's, with no shadows anywhere. 'I was walking down towards the cottages. It was very early. Mr Onions was going to work and Mrs Onions came down to the gate to see him off. She turned to go back in, and then she saw me behind the wall. I couldn't get away from her. She leapt on me and called me a poor little thing — I suppose I was damp with dew or something, and pale and cold — and she dragged me in.'

'Dragged you in? Mrs Onions?'

'Well, I suppose I could have got away. But I was curious, and so lonely. Before I knew where I was, she'd got me inside and changed my clothes and fed me. I kept telling myself I'd go next time she turned her back, but I liked the ticking clock and the smell of fire and food, and the warmth, and by the time she'd rubbed me with a towel I wasn't afraid of human hands any more. I don't know what happened then. I think I slept . . .'

'And all the time the blood was moving through your veins and you were changing?'

'Well, yes, I suppose so. I looked at myself before we came down this morning. I couldn't recognize the boy I saw. She asked me if I had anywhere else to go and I shrugged and she said, "You can be our boy, then. Mine and Mr Onions'. You can stay with us. We'll call you Jim."'

'I wanted to be warm too,' Bonnie said. 'And stay in the same place for ever, and belong.'

'We've both got what we wanted, then.'

'I don't want to go back to how things were. Not ever.'

'Nor do I.'

'I don't want to even *talk* about where we came from.'

'Nor do I . . .'

The table was heavy with decorated, glazed ham pies, and huge bowls of salad, and crusty rolls, and slices of cold lamb and beef, and steaming baked potatoes, dripping with butter. Bonnie stood looking at it all. There were voices behind her. Visitors were coming through.

She stared between the long candles at the blackberry and plum tarts with their criss-crossed latticed tops, and the jugs of thick cream, and the huge cake that Mum had made this morning. She didn't want them to come in. She didn't want to share it. What had Mum said, out in the orchard? She looked at the chains of elderberries and leaves, strung up between the beams, making extraordinary shadows in the candlelight . . . 'Sometimes I want to make time stand still.' That was what she'd said.

The door burst open behind her. Dad led everybody in. There was a rush of conversation and the room was suddenly full. 'Ah, Bonnie,' said Dad, pushing towards her. 'You sit over here.' He led her to the table and sat her down. 'You look lovely,' he said. Then he was away again, showing all the others where to sit.

Bonnie settled herself. She wore Arabella's long party frock. She felt like one of the ancestors in the paintings on the stairs. She fiddled with Godda's necklace, which she still, strangely, couldn't get off. The frock framed it perfectly against her neck and if sometimes she asked herself why Godda hadn't wanted it back, she certainly wasn't doing so tonight. She was glad she'd got it, glad to show it off. Jim, down the table, looked at her with admiration. Evans, the grain man, smiled and said he was pleased to see her well again. She smiled, pleased with herself, and began to help herself to Mrs Onions' meat pie.

Everybody else, too, began to eat. They laughed and drank and told jokes. Mum sat in the soft light at the end of the table, beaming upon them all. Dad sat at the far end where the wine was kept. His jokes were the worst of them all; Bonnie had never seen him sparkle so. In what seemed like no time at all, the cream jugs were empty and the latticed tarts were gone and the logs had burned low and new logs had been piled onto the fire. Mum lit fresh candles. Arabella had blackberry juice on the end of her nose. The laughter now was waning.

Conversations murmured quietly. Then Dad got up and made his speech.

'I think I might have drunk a bit too much,' he said. 'I think we all have, but we've got so much to celebrate.'

He looked round at them all. Mum sat back behind the candles. Her face was soft in the warm light. Everyone became very quiet.

'It's been a good year,' Dad said. 'We've had the best harvest for years. The flock's in good shape. We won some prizes at the Show. But there's more than that. Much more . . .'

He looked down the table. His eyes rested on Arabella, on Bonnie, on Florence, who had crawled into Mrs Onions' lap, on Mum. 'Where the old farms are falling into disrepair,' he said, 'and the old ways are dying and the young folk all go away to work in the cities and only the old ones are left, we've got young blood. We've got young life. We've seen the safe birth of Florence. She's even walking now. We've seen the coming of Bonnie, and now of Jim too. We've watched Arabella blossom forth with all the benefits of friends at last. And, to add to all of this, we're waiting for another child in the spring.'

Mum smiled at him. He reached for his glass and lifted it. Mum got to her feet and lifted her glass as well. 'God bless the children!' Dad said, eyes fixed on Mum.

'God bless them all!' Mum said.

They drank, and their eyes never left each other's faces, and there was not a person at the table who would have joined with them. This toast was just for them. Then Dad lifted his glass again.

'God bless Highholly Hill!'

They all clattered to their feet.

'God bless you all!' said Mum.

Their glasses rang against each other as they repeated the words and drank the toast. Then they all fell back into their seats. Only Mr Onions remained standing. He wore a dark, ill-fitting best suit. Bonnie thought she'd never really looked at him before. He had soft grey hair in a thatch all over his head and a drooping moustache and huge, calloused hands, which looked strangely out of place beneath his narrow shoulders.

'I'll sing you a song,' he said.

He folded his huge hands over his chest and closed his eyes. Bonnie expected something rough and tuneless and strong, but the fragrance of his song rose like smoke and curled around the shadowy beams and lingered long after the words had gone. Her eyes filled with unexpected tears. It was a perfect ending to the supper. His voice was sweet, and fresh as roses.

23

The last of the summer days tumbled like ripe plums, and everything changed. Dry leaves fluttered down the fields into heaps along the bottoms of hedges. Days became darker and shorter, and patches of dank, cool fog crept into the valley. Dad ploughed and did his winter planting. He pulled up decaying garden debris and lit huge bonfires of the stuff in the orchard.

Mum began school lessons again. Now she had a class of three, for Jim came down and joined them. 'You can't even *read*,' Mum would say. 'I can't understand it. You don't know *anything*. It's as if you've never been taught. You're such a bright boy, too.'

On good afternoons, after school, they'd run with him up as far as Roundhill, and wave him off as he blew down the other side. On wet, cold days, they'd sit with him in the inglenook and read to him, and draw and play and listen to the wind outside. Some days, it blew so hard and angrily that the whole house shook. Soot blustered down chimneys and the wind got under doors and through cracks in window-frames. It lifted carpets, shook curtains, forced them all to huddle between the stone walls of the inglenook while blast after blast hit the house like waves against a shore.

Some nights Bonnie would lie awake and listen to the wind. She'd pull the curtains back and watch arthritic trees tremble violently. She'd hear branches creak all over the hill, hear them crash down. She'd wonder how Highholly House took it all, how it still stood there, year after year, against such batterings.

Then the weather would change. The fog would come down, not like the delicate mists of summertime, with their pastel shades and mysterious shapes, or even the dank coolness of autumn mornings, but lifelessly, murkily, a nasty blanket that settled upon house and hill and wouldn't go away again for days.

Then, unexpectedly, the sky would become clear and freezing blue and Bonnie would feel as if she could reach up and put a finger on it and it would crack like icy puddles and there would be jagged patterns all over it. There would be sunrises that took her breath away. The meadows would creak with frost and Dad would ferry in provisions, in case of snow. Jim would slither down the ice-encrusted meadow for school, on polythene sacks. He'd look like a huge sack himself, wrapped from head to foot in layers of clothing, with his pinched, steaming face hardly showing at all.

It was really winter now. Mrs Onions helped with Christmas cakes and puddings. Mum conducted lessons, sitting in a chair with a cushion against her back and her feet up on a small stool and her hands folded over the growing bulge that took over her lap. After lunch, Mum would go to bed and Jim would go home or the three of them would run together up the hill, to play.

'Let's go up to the Throne,' Arabella said, one restless, boding, blustery afternoon. They flung on their coats.

'Why don't you take Jake?' Mrs Onions said. 'No one seems to want to take him out any more.'

They shook their heads and rushed away.

'Poor Jake,' she said, but the dog never looked at her. And she didn't know why, but she didn't really like him either, any more.

They climbed up to the top. Arabella, carried by the wind, rushed ahead. Jim struggled. His cheeks were red with exertion and he shivered and wrapped his coat round himself more tightly. The wind beat at the back of his head and his hair blew into his eyes. 'I can't stand it,' he said. 'I feel so cold.'

Bonnie, blowing up behind him, laughed. 'Arabella says that this is nothing. She says it'll get a lot worse before the winter's through.'

'I never used to feel cold or hot. The wind never pushed me over. I didn't used to feel a thing.'

'It's the price of being human,' Bonnie teased. She looked up. Above them, at the Throne, Arabella had already found the crack between the rocks. Bonnie remembered the deep drop on the other side.

'We all ought to stay together,' she said. 'Come on!'

When they got to the Throne, Arabella had disappeared. Bonnie found the crack between the rocks, and squeezed her way in. 'Arabella!' she called anxiously. But the wind whipped her voice away, and there was no reply. The wind seemed to slice in, even through this secret crack between the rocks. She struggled against it all the way, till they came out on the white, smooth stone where Edric was meant to sit above the valley.

'There you are,' she said, in some relief. 'You're all right. I was worried the wind might blow you over the edge.'

Arabella stood, alone and thoughtful. The high stone walls of the Throne helped keep the wind at bay. It was unexpectedly quiet and still.

'Do you think they really helped us?' she said. 'Perhaps I shouldn't say it up here, but we could have imagined it.'

Bonnie felt the necklace beneath her coat. 'They seem so far away now,' she said. 'Even up here, they seem so far away.' She shivered. 'Just like the summer.'

'I always hope I might see them up here, but I never do,' Arabella said. A great gust of wind rushed over the top of the stones, and nearly knocked her down. 'I even wonder, despite everything, if they're really real,' she said.

Jim struggled out of the crack after them. 'I've never felt so cold. I can't stand it. I can't bear it up here. I'm going home.'

'There's nothing to do up here. I don't know why we came. It *is* cold. We'll go too,' Arabella said.

They parted ways where the sheep's path forked for Roundhill. Bonnie and Arabella struggled, against the wind now, down towards the holly grove. At Batholes, Arabella stopped. Its mouth yawned even wider and darker now that the brambles had all died back.

'I always think I know only half the hill,' she said, wistfully. 'I always think this is the gateway to all sorts of secrets, that there's a *world* down there. We'd find all sorts of things if you'd only come with me.'

Bonnie looked up into the sky, where low, dark clouds were gathering. The necklace, for the first time in a long while, stung, and she pulled it out and eased her finger around her neck. 'I'd never want to shut myself away in the dark where there's no sky,' she said. 'Let's get back, shall we?'

On the brow of Roundhill, Jim waved to them. They waved back and he disappeared. Arabella looked at the dark clouds. The wind was dropping. She could imagine them settling. She tore herself away from Batholes' dark entrance. 'Oh, all right,' she sighed.

They climbed over the top gate into the field and made their way down to the holly grove. The wind was almost gone now and they didn't have to struggle any more. It was cold as ever. The girls followed the path between the first of the hollies.

'Someone's been here.' Bonnie pushed ahead of Arabella, between the branches.

'What?' Arabella said.

'Look,' said Bonnie. 'Look down there.'

They looked. Two pits had been dug. One was shallow, the other was deep. In the deep pit, logs had been stacked and covered with polythene, to keep them dry.

'Someone's been collecting logs, that's all,' Arabella said. 'I expect it was Dad. Why are you looking like that?'

Bonnie couldn't speak. A picture, so clear and real that it could have been projected right across the sky, had come into her mind. It was a summer picture, with long grass fresh and growing, and birds singing. It was a picture not of Dad but of the other Michael, digging the firepit in front of the flint-faced house. Of the shadowboy stoking the fire . . .

'Come on,' Arabella said. 'It's getting dreadfully dark. Look at those clouds. It's only a pile of sticks.'

Numbly, Bonnie followed Arabella along the path between the pits and right through the clearing to the other side. Her mind was spinning. 'He wouldn't do it again, would he?' she thought. 'He's not the shadowboy. He's Jim and he wants to stay here. Arabella must be right. It'll have been Dad or Mr Onions, collecting logs.'

Dad was in the kitchen, brewing a cup of tea. Mum, of course, was up in bed, and Mrs Onions said she'd have to go soon; she had things to do at home.

'It's raw out there,' said Dad. 'You'd best wrap up before you go.'

Mrs Onions left and Bonnie opened her mouth to ask about the pits. The necklace stung her neck and she pulled at it unhappily. Before she could speak, Dad turned to them both.

'Does either of you know anything about that old, broken mirror in the hedge down the track?'

Bonnie froze. It was as though time, everything, had stopped. She couldn't feel a thing. She shut her mouth again.

'Seems a good mirror,' Dad went on. 'Gilt frame and all. I thought I might get it out and bring it up. It seems a waste down there. It's not even been put so we can see if things come round the bend. It's useless really. All you can see is the track up to the house.'

'A . . . a mirror?' Arabella stuttered, somewhere in a

153

24

'The clouds have really got us this time,' said Dad. They were in the living-room and tea was over and he'd got up to draw the curtains. 'The wind's dropped just like that. Look at it.'

The girls looked. There was nothing to see beyond the edge of the yard. No twinkling lights across the valley. Nothing.

'You'd think that nothing existed beyond those fence posts, wouldn't you?' Dad said to Bonnie. 'That's what comes of living on a hill. We get stuck in every wretched low cloud that comes along. Specially at this time of year.' He drew the curtains. 'Will you two be all right? I've got accounts to do tonight and Mum's gone up already. Have you got something to do?'

'Yes,' said the girls together.

'I'll go and get on, then.'

As soon as he'd gone, the girls rushed through the house and out into the scullery to find their coats and boots. They struggled with the scullery door and tiptoed out onto the terrace. It was murky, damp, still bitterly cold. They padded like slinky farm cats down the yard and climbed over the farmyard gate, and already they could see hardly anything of the house. They took a few steps down the bumpy track, and they couldn't even see the gate. They could have been anywhere. Apart from a few cold sheep, curled up among the roots of hawthorn hedges, they were alone.

'We'll be all right,' Arabella said. 'We're safe as long as we stay on the track.'

Bonnie followed her along the top and then down towards the Dingle. She didn't feel safe, because the necklace tingled round her neck. She knew she wouldn't feel safe again until they'd found the mirror, hidden it, destroyed it, done *something* to it. She followed Arabella past blackberry hedges and dead elders and rowans and hawthorns, in what seemed a never-ending journey. Everything looked the same. Her hands became numb. The cloud never seemed to lighten. It was as if they took it with them.

'It feels,' she thought, 'as if we've been out here ten years.' Her face felt raw and cold. Her ears hurt. Her nose was sore and her neck, beneath the necklace, hurt. She didn't want to find the mirror. She didn't want ever to see it again. And she was angry with herself for not having realized Grandmother Marvell would be back. She should have known.

At last they dipped between the banks of the twisty canyon. The trees of Hope Dingle surrounded them. Bonnie stumbled after Arabella's disappearing back, tripped on the deep ruts of the track.

'Wait for me, Arabella!'

Arabella waited, eyes sliding from side to side, while Bonnie caught up.

'We must be near it now,' Bonnie shivered. There was something eerie in the greyness of the Dingle. 'It must be somewhere in the hedge down here. We must be careful.' She remembered Jake, the old, real Jake, and that awful door with its glint of mirror behind it, and the way he'd tumbled in. '*We could walk into it if we're not careful . . .* '

Arabella shivered too. 'I can't see anything,' she whispered. And why was she whispering? Who did she think might be down here?

'You look that side,' Bonnie said, nodding at the trees. 'I'll look over here.'

They crept forward again, stumbled round a bend in the track. There was no mirror to be seen. The track plunged deeper. Now they heard the brook below them. The track took another turn. The white bridge loomed ahead of them. There was still no mirror.

'We must have missed it.' Arabella frowned. 'Dad *did* say in the hedge, didn't he?'

'Sshh . . . ' said Bonnie.

'What?'

'SSHH . . . '

Bonnie was tilting her head. Something was bothering her. Her gaze slid in and out among thick, dead brambles and a tangle of young hazel trees. Nothing stirred except the brook which rushed noisily beneath the bridge, down towards the valley.

'Look there.'

The nose of a car peeped out at them, between the bushes. Its lights were off. They were almost upon the thing and yet they could have walked past it in the murky gloom and never have noticed that it was there.

Arabella huddled close to Bonnie's side.

'It's all right,' Bonnie whispered. 'It's empty.'

They crept closer. Bonnie recognized the car. It was the rattly machine Grandmother Marvell had driven up the hill. She'd have recognized it anywhere. It was just like Grandbag's cars.

'She must be here somewhere . . . '

Looking around her, she could see nothing but the car, and the track beneath her feet, and bits of overhanging branches, and the nearest end of the bridge. Beyond that narrow little world, Grandmother Marvell could be anywhere. The mirror could be anywhere.

'I don't like it, Bonnie. Let's go.'

'I don't like it either. But we haven't found the mirror. We've got to take it down. We've got . . . we've got to hide it, break it, throw it in the brook. We've got to get rid of it!'

'But where is it?'

'Maybe it's the other side of the brook.'

They considered the bridge uncomfortably. The canyon walls rose up on either side of it. Grandmother Marvell's eyes could be on them even now. Up above them. Among the trees. Between some gap in the hedge. Behind the car. Over the brook . . .

'Come on.'

They edged onto the bridge. The brook was full now with winter water that drained off the hill. It rushed noisily beneath them while they crept forward. Bonnie rubbed her neck uncomfortably. She couldn't see the end of the bridge. Unpleasant things could be waiting for them over there. She inched forward, Arabella at her side. Then she saw the far end and a bit of clear and empty track that rose beyond it with nobody in sight.

They came off the bridge and began to search among the trees and hedgerows. There was no mirror to be seen.

'It wasn't over here,' Arabella said. 'We've missed it. Dad said — don't you remember — he said it pointed up the hill to the house.'

'Of course.'

They turned to go back over the bridge. Then Godda's necklace bit at Bonnie's neck and Bonnie stopped. Arabella whispered, 'We can't go back that way. There's someone waiting for us at the other end. I can feel the eyes . . .'

'I can feel them too,' Bonnie whispered back. She looked round helplessly. '*I don't know what to do.*'

Arabella looked around her. She put a finger over her lips and pointed down among the ghosts of trees.

'What?' whispered Bonnie.

'We'll go down there.'

'Down where?'

'Underneath the bridge. Over the brook. Up the other side. We'll go back up to the house across the fields. She'll never find us if she's waiting on the track.'

Bonnie listened to the rushing brook. She shivered. She couldn't think of anything else to do, but she didn't want to wade through the fast-flowing water.

'She'll hear us,' she whispered, searching for an excuse not to go. 'And like you said, we're only safe if we stay on the track. We'll get lost if we try to cut across the fields.'

'Better lost than caught,' Arabella hissed back. 'And she won't hear us. The brook's so loud, she'll never hear a thing.'

'We haven't found the mirror yet.'

'And we're not going to, with her sitting on the track.' Arabella began to squeeze through the hedge, and cut down between the trees. 'We don't have any choice,' was the last thing Bonnie heard.

She followed her. They did have a choice, of course. But what a choice it was! The thought of Grandmother Marvell's eyes settling gleefully on them again made shudders run up and down Bonnie's whole body. She pushed down the soft bank in Arabella's wake, ducking and diving under and between branches while the sound of the brook became louder and closer. Suddenly she saw the brook and, rising out of it, the white posts of the bridge.

'This is the place,' Arabella mouthed. 'I've crossed here lots of times. It's all right in the summer.'

But it wasn't summer now. Bonnie heard Arabella gasp as she slid into the icy water, and then bite back the gasp as if afraid, despite everything, that someone might hear her. She followed after her. She was quite unprepared for the brook's depth. Two steps and she was up to her waist. The water that rushed at her was so strong it nearly knocked her over. Two steps more and she collided with Arabella. They clung to each other and stumbled forward, gasping at every step. Suddenly they found themselves sinking in soft mud. Bonnie hauled desperately. Her reluctant boot, with accompanying sucking noises, came out clear and she secured it upon a solid, flat stone while she dragged the other foot free.

'I'm stuck,' Arabella cried. 'I'm sinking.'

Bonnie turned. Arabella was up to her chest. Desperately, she pulled and tugged at her and suddenly Arabella came free, without her wellingtons. They both fell backwards, onto the bank.

'Your boots!' Bonnie said.

'Never mind them. Let's get away.'

They tried to climb up the bank towards the fields. But their hands, as they reached out, shook so much that they could hardly lift themselves. Arabella's teeth chattered violently. Bonnie's were hardly any quieter. Arabella bit back her cries as her bare feet stubbed against tree roots and sharp stones.

At last they came out of the trees, into a field. 'If we go up there,' Arabella said, between her shaking teeth, 'if we go up straight, we should find a stile into the next field and, if we go up straight again, we should come out onto the track beneath the house.'

They began to climb. The field was ploughed and the soil clung to Arabella's feet, weighing them down and making it harder still for her to move. Bonnie moved more easily, but with a dreadful, squelching noise inside her boots that she was sure Grandmother Marvell could hear two fields away. They still couldn't see a thing ahead of them. They seemed to climb for hours.

'Where's that stile?' Bonnie chattered through blue lips.

'We must have missed it.' Arabella was growing stiffer by the minute. She kept falling down and it hurt her to get up again. 'We can't have walked straight after all,' she said. 'We must be going round and round in circles. I can't even find the hedge.'

'What's that?' Bonnie said.

They both squinted. Distant lights flickered. They

couldn't be the lights of the house. They couldn't be the stars. They were *moving*. They couldn't be anything but . . .

'It's Grandmother Marvell, isn't it?'

They flopped onto the ground. What was the point of hiding? They were in the middle of the field. There was nowhere to go. The lights grew bigger. They were coming towards them, searching them out as if they smelt — as if they knew — where they were. The field was lit by hazy twin arcs. They'd tried so hard, and now she'd got them.

'We couldn't have stopped her anyhow,' Bonnie whispered. 'She'd have found some other way to get us in the end.'

The lights stopped. In a dream, or so it seemed, a figure stepped out in front of them. Its black bulk crunched across the grass towards them. As if to remind them of what they soon would be, the Jake-thing, sleek and cold, with empty, bored, dead eyes, slunk down by its side.

'Well, blast me, what have we here?'

The voice woke them from the freezing, awful dream. They recognized the Land Rover's engine running. It was Dad.

25

Bonnie and Arabella sat tucked up in their beds, drinking down the last of their cocoa. Their teeth had stopped chattering. Their skin had changed to pink again. Dad hovered by the light switch.

'You haven't really explained what you were doing,' he said.

They both thought of Mum, asleep and nursing her growing bulge, and knew they couldn't explain. Anything might happen if they worried her. They had to sort this out on their own. The doctor said they had to be so very careful with her . . .

'We . . . we just wanted a walk,' Bonnie said, lamely.

'We got lost,' said Arabella.

'We're sorry, Dad.'

'Really we are.'

'We won't do it again.'

'You'd better not,' said Dad, in a voice that had to be taken seriously. 'You didn't even keep to the path. I don't know what came over you. I won't tell Mum this time, and you won't *ever* be so silly again.'

He turned out the light. 'Goodnight,' he said. They heard his footsteps fading along the corridor and down the stairs.

'We haven't got the mirror,' Bonnie said, bleakly.

'She's out there somewhere.'

'We were fools to think she'd gone. We should have been prepared for this. We should have known. Even if we get the mirror, that won't stop her. She's just like

Grandbag. She'll always think of something else.'

'What'll we do, Bonnie?'

'I don't know.' Despite her anxiety, Bonnie yielded her face to the softness of her pillow. She wriggled down the bed and felt her tired limbs melting in the warmth.

'I think we should hope that Edric's real,' came Arabella's anxious voice. 'He's all we've got. I think we should go and look for him. We could go down Batholes. If he's anywhere, he's meant to be down there. The miners used to say they could hear him knocking. It's supposed to be his job, Bonnie, to look after the hill.'

Distantly, Bonnie remembered herself climbing out of the attic window. She remembered her heart beating and the jump. Those hands as soft as angels' wings — *had* they been real? Was there really an Edric, a Godda, who guarded the hill? She thought of Batholes, yawning blackly, even on the brightest day. She slunk further down the bed.

'I've done one horrid thing tonight. I'm not doing another.'

Suddenly, even thinking about Grandmother Marvell out on the hill couldn't worry her any more. The warmth and softness of the bed lulled her. She'd had a hard night. Waves of exhaustion, that she'd held at bay, broke over her now. Arabella's voice was so distant . . .

Arabella woke up. The remains of Dad's cocoa lay beside the bed. She stared through the dark. Everything was very quiet and she didn't know what had woken her. The glassy eyes of the dolls on the mantelpiece glinted at her. The bulk of Bonnie breathed up and down beneath a mountain of bedcovers. An owl fluttered, swooping close to the house and then away again. Its cry echoed through the night. It was the anxious, warning noise the owls made when foxes were round the henhouse.

Perhaps that was what had woken her? She waited for the sound of Dad next door. Waited for the click of the light and the opening of the bedroom window and the thump of the shotgun as he positioned it in readiness. But she heard none of these sounds. She heard something above her in the dark instead. What was it? She heard it again. Where was it coming from? Was it over Bonnie's bed? It was hard to tell in the darkness. It was a scratching, scuffling noise. It was in the attic. That was it. In the attic above the wardrobe.

'It's nothing to worry about,' she whispered to herself. 'It's only mice.'

'No, it's not.'

She jumped and stared at the shape beneath the mound of covers. Bonnie's eyes stared back at her.

'You're awake,' Arabella said.

'The necklace woke me up,' Bonnie said. 'It really hurts and it doesn't do that for mice, does it?'

'You mean . . . ?'

'Grandmother Marvell's in the attic.'

'Grandmother . . . ?'

'Scratching with her fingernails.'

As she spoke, they heard a a gnawing, picking sound. Pick, pick, pick, up in the ceiling. Much too loud and strong for mice. It seemed to reach out for them through the darkness of the half-opened wardrobe door.

'Don't be ridiculous.' Arabella dropped her voice. 'Of course she isn't up there. There's no way she could . . .'

A chunk of plaster fell inside the wardrobe. It may have been a small piece, but it sounded very large and loud.

'You know what she's doing, don't you?' Bonnie whispered back to her. 'She's got her mirror up there. Listen. She's trying to make a hole that's big enough to get it down. She'll put it at the end of the bed or inside the wardrobe or over the dressing-table mirror . . .'

'Stop it, Bonnie. Stop it right away. It's because it's dark. It's only mice. It's because we're tired and everything seems bigger and worse. She could never get up there. She could never get a mirror like that up there.'

'Like she could never get an old car up the track? She did it, Arabella. She brought it right up into the yard, with that huge mirror on top of it. She can do things, Arabella.'

'You're just imagining it, Bonnie. You're tired. It's only mice. Dad'll go up in the morning and put poison down. He'll send the cats up. I'll shut the wardrobe door. That'll make us both feel better. And then . . . '

'And then?' Bonnie watched as Arabella scrambled out of bed.

'Well, we're awake again. We could talk again. We've got to make a plan, haven't we?'

Arabella padded across the floor. But when she came to the wardrobe door, something came over her. What was it? Curiosity? The need to prove, so they could sleep again, that Bonnie was really wrong? She opened the wardrobe door wider and peered inside.

'Arabella, don't!'

It was pitch dark. She pulled the coats and dresses aside and stepped into the wardrobe. Her feet fell over the fallen plaster. She fumbled between more clothes. Why, she'd forgotten about half these dresses. She looked up. She couldn't see a hole up there, not even a little glimmer of an attic beyond. But, reflected, she could see herself . . .

Bonnie heard the stifled scream. She heard hangers flying, dresses falling everywhere. Then there was silence. Not even scratching any more. Just silence.

'Arabella, are you all right?'

There was no answer.

'Arabella!'

She got out of bed. Cautiously tiptoed to the wardrobe door. Opened it and looked inside. She could see nothing. *Nothing*. 'Arabella!' she called again, but no one answered her and no one moved. She stepped inside and put out her hand. 'It's me. It's Bonnie. You're all right . . . '

She began to feel about. No one was there. *No one was there*! She felt the wardrobe from side to side. No one was there . . .

Suddenly, she heard a sound above her head. Like a flash of inspiration, unexpected, like those hands that *had* saved her once, the words came into her head: *Don't look up*.

She stood very still. She heard the dragging sound of something heavy being pulled away. Something like a mirror in an ornamental frame. It faded, and she stood in the silence and knew what had happened. There was a hole in the ceiling above her head. She didn't need to look to see it there, or to imagine the mirror laid across it and Arabella sucked up into it . . .

Grandmother Marvell had won. Grandbag had won too. You couldn't run away from the clutching grasp of hate and greed. Arabella was gone.

26

Bonnie climbed over Arabella's bed and looked up the hill. Low, nasty clouds still swirled outside the window and her mind went to the darkness of Batholes. She thought of crawling down there, shutting herself away beneath the soft skin of the body of the earth, discovering its secrets, not like the busy surgeon with his knife, but like the shocked layman who never knew all those passages, tunnels, chambers, orifices, were even there . . . She shuddered. She didn't want to go. But what choice was there? What else could she do? She peered through the clouds, towards the holly grove.

'There's a choice up there,' she said to herself.

'What do you mean?' she replied.

'I don't know . . . '

She got off the bed again, and dressed in warm layers, topped with waterproofs. Then she crept through the house to the kitchen. Cream cats stirred and stared at her, but the sleeping, uncaring Jake-thing never moved. She found the torch on the pantry shelf, and spare batteries. She saw a block of cooking chocolate and imagined the need she'd have in some nasty passageway for comfort and sustenance, and she took that too.

'*There is another choice*,' something inside her said again.

'What do you mean?'

'*It's in the holly grove . . .*'

'I don't know what you mean.'

'*Oh yes you do . . .*'

Out on the hill, the fog was thick as ever. As Bonnie felt her way up through the orchard, memories crowded in. Mum collecting plums, Florence crawling in the long, summer grass, Mum telling them about another baby, Jake bounding happily between the trees and Arabella chasing him . . .

She climbed over the stile into the meadow. It was like the old days, being on her own again. But it seemed so strange. She'd become used to doing things with Arabella. Her feet found the ridges of the sheep's path. She began to feel her way along it, hurriedly. Did Jake and Arabella still exist somewhere beyond that awful mirror? Were they dead, or would they come back? Even if she found Edric and Godda, could they really help? Or was it too late?

'Oh, where are you, Arabella? What are you going through now? What are you feeling?'

She came to the outer hollies of the grove. A thud caught her attention. She paused. A branch shook. It was a sheep, of course, caught up, as they so often were, its long fleece tangled in the holly leaves. She climbed, taking care herself not to get caught, between the branches into the grove. She felt again the stillness and strangeness of the holly grove. It was not a sheep. She let out a cry.

'Jim!'

A trench had been dug between the pits. Staves had been erected. Jim was breaking fresh logs for the pile. So wrapped up was he in what he did that he hadn't noticed her approach. Her voice made him drop a log and flush, not like a flickering shadowboy, but like a human one.

'What are you doing?' Bonnie said.

He looked terribly ashamed. 'I don't know.'

'You dug these pits, didn't you?'

He hung his head.

'And you did all this?'

'I don't want to go back,' he said. 'I don't want *you* to go. I don't know why I did it. I don't understand. I

169

just had to. I couldn't sleep. I had to come here. I had to do it.'

Bonnie stooped over the firepit. She wanted to pull all the logs out, throw them everywhere, scatter them away. Distantly, she heard Jim's voice saying 'I'm sorry' over and over again. But she couldn't answer him. Something was struggling at the back of her mind. What was it, oh what was it?

Surprised at herself, she began to cry. She thought of Arabella lost, and the pain that Mum was going to feel. She thought of the whole hill in danger and herself crawling down into the one place in the whole, huge world she'd never choose to go.

Jim came to her. He put his arms right round her and held her tight. He didn't feel like a shadowboy. It was as if he really was a son of Mrs Onions. Just the way she would have behaved. He didn't seem embarrassed at all, as you'd expect boys to be. He didn't seem bothered. He just crouched there and held Bonnie tight for a long, long time of crying, and then Bonnie said, 'I know what's been struggling at the back of my mind. I've known it all along. It was me who triggered Grandmother Marvell's arrival. You won't understand, I'm not sure I do either, but it's as if she came for me but found Arabella instead. I thought that, when I first saw her. I remember now. It's as if my coming's turned all this into, oh, I don't know, some kind of mirror world . . . There's another me, another Michael, another Maybelle. There had to be another Grandbag too. And I've got a feeling that if I went back home, everything here would be all right again. Grandmother Marvell would release Arabella and Jake. She wouldn't *belong* here any more. She'd have to go away.' She looked around her at the logs. 'I think that's why you're doing all this. Because you know. Somehow you know that I've got to go.'

'I don't know what you're talking about.'

'Nor do I.'

170

'I don't want either of us to have to go.'

'Nor do I, Jim, nor do I . . . '

Bonnie wiped her tears away. Incongruously, she remembered the cooking chocolate in her pocket. She got it out and broke it up and offered some to Jim and ate the rest herself. It comforted her. It gave her what she needed to raise her head and look around. There were no clouds in the holly grove. Everything was clear. But she could feel the foggy darkness out there, waiting. The darkness of that distant home she'd left behind, or the darkness of Batholes . . .

'I'm going to try the other way first,' she said — amazed that she was choosing Batholes when there was another way. 'I won't go unless I *have* to. I won't give up Highholly Hill, unless there's *really* no other way.'

'What can I do?' Jim said.

She wiped the crumbs of chocolate away. 'Do you really mean it?'

'Of course I do.'

'And do you really mean that you want to stay?'

He looked around at the pits he'd dug and the things he'd done. 'It doesn't look like it,' he said. 'But yes, of course . . . '

'Then come with me.'

'Come with you where?'

Bonnie brushed her sticky hands against her waterproof. She felt the bulge of the torch in her pocket and she couldn't bring herself even to say the name of the place.

'Come on. I'll show you.'

He followed her out into the swirling night. They climbed up through the top meadow and over the gate. They found the sheep's path again, between the bracken. Every sound in the fog, a sheep running away, a stone dislodged, a distant farm dog somewhere barking, sounded a hundred times louder. The ground smelt raw and dank. Suddenly they found themselves at Batholes.

The warning notice loomed out of the gloom and Bonnie almost fell over it.

'There,' she said, looking at the black hole beyond the notice. 'There you are. It's the only hope we've got. You won't understand and I don't know how to explain it all, but Arabella's gone and we've got to find Wild Edric — and if he's anywhere, he's down in there.'

She shivered. Jim looked up from the hole into the cloudy sky. 'If we don't find him,' he said, 'then it's back up there for us. Back home. Back to how things used to be.'

'That's right,' she said. She scrambled over the mess of brambles in the cave's mouth. Got out her torch and flashed it into the dark. Suddenly everything felt so unreal. So dreamlike. This couldn't be her, could it, embarking on this ridiculous thing?

'I don't want to, but I've got to, haven't I? Will you come with me?'

'Yes,' said Jim.

27

They both tore down the spiders' webs that festooned themselves like strings of pearls across the entrance. Barring the way were the bones of a dead sheep. Bonnie stepped around it, with a slight shudder. Batholes' roof sloped steeply down. She stooped. Her torch shook as she got onto hands and knees. She crawled forward. The dark hole seemed to suck her in like a hungry mouth, and she crawled on and suddenly she knew that the sky and the great open world weren't behind her any more. That she was *underground*.

The hole turned into a long, thin tunnel. It turned sharply downwards and narrowed some more. There was no way she could turn. No way of getting out again unless she came out backwards. She wanted to be out, but Jim, behind her, blocked her escape. She could hear him breathe. She wanted to be sick.

'You've got a torch, haven't you?' he said.

'Of course I've got a torch!'

'Well, hold it steady, then!'

His human, boy's voice comforted her. She held the torch up, so that the light cut through a misty atmosphere. The ground beneath her was cold and muddy. The rocks shone with the hidden moisture of the hill. The tunnel sloped downwards.

'I think it gets a bit wider down there,' Bonnie said, and her words came out in damp clouds of condensation. 'I hope it does. I feel like the weight of the whole hill's on my back. I feel like I can't breathe . . .'

They crawled downwards and the ground beneath them became boggier. Bonnie was glad of her waterproofs, but even through her several gloves her hands became numb. She found it hard to crawl with the torch in one hand. The roof of the passage sloped towards the floor and she realized, with horror, that she was going to have to lie down in the mud in order to get along. What would happen if the passage continued sloping down? Would they be able to slide up again? Would they — again she wanted to be sick — would they get stuck?

She lay down in the mud and it was the worst moment in her whole life. She began to slide downwards through it. She realized she'd made a mistake. She should have gone feet first. All the blood pumped to her head. The roof came down lower. The passage became steeper. Then, when she thought that she could bear no more, it opened out. The roof rose starkly. The walls on either side of her were swept away.

'Oh, Jim, oh . . . '

She rolled, gasping and unprepared, into a huge, quietly dripping, terrifying void. Jim rolled after her. She caught his face in her torchlight. He too was breathless and his eyes bulged and his whole face was bright with the rush of blood, but he began to look around excitedly, peering through the thin beam of Bonnie's torch.

'It's *beautiful*,' he said. 'Look at those rocks. They're all wet. They look so clean. And look . . . ' He directed the torchlight. 'Look at those drops of water in the air. They look like jewels.'

Bonnie sat up and stared dejectedly. She wanted to cry, because it wasn't beautiful at all. It was awful. It was *all* awful, and she wanted to get out of it. She thought of Godda and Edric and her heart went out to them. She'd rather die than have to live down here. She almost hoped, for their sakes, that they weren't real after all. If they were, how did they manage it? Did they sleep down here through the centuries till they were needed above the ground? Did rocks encase them, hold them fast? Were there fossil marks where their beds had been? Did Godda look at the blue enamel sky, at the diamond stars of her necklace, and long for the open air again? Did she miss her precious necklace, now that it was fixed, as tight as ever, round Bonnie's neck?

Oh, it was hard, now that she could see the squalid inside of the earth, hard to believe that anything could live down here among the wet rocks and the blackness. Bonnie listened bleakly. There was no tap, tap, tapping, like the miners used to say they heard. No shaking of the ground. Nothing.

Nothing? She strained to listen. *Something* was there. What was it?

'I can hear it too,' Jim said. 'I think it's water.'

'Water?'

'A river or something. Let's go and see.'

Bonnie shone the torch up through the void. Jim stepped forward and she followed him. The mud beneath their feet turned into a stream. They splashed through it. Water oozed out of the rocks all around them. The sound ahead of them grew louder, and Bonnie took Jim's hand.

'At least we haven't got to crawl any more,' Jim comforted.

'But how long for?' Bonnie replied. The void was narrowing into a passageway again. She didn't like the way those rocks closed in. They turned a corner. Suddenly the rushing sound was very loud and close. It sounded like a torrent's roar. Bonnie had a picture of them both, swept away in the path of a great, unbounding, underground river. She turned to run, but Jim held her tight.

'Look Bonnie, look . . . It's all right. Look!'

He got her hand with the torch in it, and pointed the beam. Ahead, in the thin light, the stream became a dark pool into which a huge, white, foaming waterfall fell.

'Oh!' cried Bonnie.

175

It was like an unexpected wedding veil hanging in the dark back of the wardrobe, a ballerina's frock flickering upon a television screen.

'You can't say *that's* not beautiful,' Jim said.

Bonnie stood transfixed. She couldn't, could she? Then, as if one shock wasn't enough, a fleck of something fluttered out of the dark at her. She caught it briefly in the torch light, then it struck her cheek and flew away again. An albino moth!

'Oh . . . ' said Bonnie again. Hope stirred within her. Maybe Edric and Godda were down here, after all. There *was* life in this place. There *was* beauty. There could be hope . . .

'Come on,' Jim said.

They waded round the edge of the pool and followed the river path on its other side. The passage was long and thin again. Even shining the torch up high, they couldn't see a roof to it.

'A great, long crack in the ground . . . '

'I wonder what bit of hill we're under now?'

The passage sloped up. The stream slid away from them. They found themselves squelching through mud again, and realized that the walls on either side of them were folding in over their heads. Bits of rock seemed to have become dislodged and fallen in their path. They found themselves scrambling. The passage, like a roller-coaster, plunged back down. They found more boulders, turned a corner, and stopped. The way was blocked with a great pile of stones. As Bonnie looked at it, her brief, brave hope faded again.

'We can't get through,' she said.

Jim went up close. 'Yes we can. There's a hole down there. Between the stones. It's not very big, but neither are we. There's been a fall of stones, that's all. Once we've got through, it'll be all clear again on the other side.'

Bonnie pointed her torch and found the hole and wished she hadn't. 'I can't do it,' she said.

Jim looked straight up at her, in the torch light. 'We've got to,' he said simply.

Bonnie's stomach lurched. She wanted to be sick, because he was right. She wanted to cry but instead, without a word, she got down on hands and knees and peered into the hole.

'I'll go first, if you'd like me to,' Jim said.

'Oh no,' she replied. Her voice shook. 'If you went first, I might get left behind. I mightn't be brave enough to follow you and then I'd be stuck here on my own, in the dark.'

She took a deep breath, pushed her head into the hole and started wriggling. She shifted, inch by inch and from side to side, till she was in, up to the waist. Jim touched her on the leg. 'You're doing great,' she heard him say. His voice was flat and close, but he might have been a million miles away. She was in a dark world of her own. She felt the stones around her shift and she thought, 'They're all *loose*. They're not fixed at all. I could move one of them and some great boulder would come down and crush my head or, even worse — because at least I'd be dead then and I wouldn't know any more — it could come down and trap me in here and I'd die here, slowly.'

'I'm coming out,' she called.

'What?' Jim cried.

'I'm coming back.'

She began to wriggle, but nothing seemed to move.

'Help me!'

Jim didn't seem to hear. The boulders shifted.

'HELP ME!!' she screamed again. And then she felt his hands on her legs. She felt him pulling her. She felt the whole hill, the whole, great hill upon her back. She couldn't breathe. She wriggled furiously. He pulled again. And she was out!

She lay upon the ground a long, long time, in the mud, in the slime, in the clinging cold. She couldn't speak, and a million hopes, dreams, aspirations for the

whole rest of her life on Highholly Hill faded away in
the darkness of that hole. She knew she'd never find
Wild Edric, knew she'd have to help Jim light that firepit.
Knew she'd have to make the journey back again, into
the sky.

'I can't go on,' she said.

28

'It's all right. You did your best. We'd better find our way out of here again. You were very brave,' Jim said.

She got to her feet. She was stiff with clammy mud. It seemed to have got in everywhere, through the zip of her waterproofs, into her trousers, through her gloves, in her hair . . . In the thin light of the torch she stood looking utterly wretched, and Jim reached out a hand and touched her lightly.

'You did your best,' he said again, and they smiled sadly at each other. 'Let's get out of here. That torch of yours is getting a bit faint.'

Bonnie handed it to him. 'You lead the way this time,' she said dejectedly.

They struggled together, back the way they'd come. Up and down the switchback passageway. Through the stream. Past the waterfall again. It didn't look like a bridal veil now that hope had gone. It looked like an ordinary waterfall. The air was still full of sparkling droplets, but the living, fluttering albino moth might never have been.

'Just like Edric and Godda,' Bonnie thought, and she remembered something Mum had said once. It seemed so long ago. 'Lots of people look for Edric and Godda and never find them . . . '

Suddenly the torch went out. They stood in the dripping, splashing dark. 'I've got batteries,' she heard her voice say, woodenly. 'It'll be all right.'

She unzipped her waterproof and found another battery, and she and Jim fumbled to put it in. Jim flicked the switch on, and nothing happened.

'But they're new batteries. I got them off the shelf.'

'They're wet.'

'You mean . . . '

'We'll have to *feel* our way home.'

Bonnie remembered the way up ahead, the great void in which it would be so easy to get lost, the little, narrow tunnel with its low roof which would force them to slither flat on their faces through the mud. The thought of doing such a thing in utter blackness made her shiver all over. She thought of eels and frogs and slimy things that might be up there. She thought of Grandmother Marvell loose somewhere out on the hill. What if she'd followed them in here? What if she waited somewhere up ahead, in the dark?

'Stay close behind,' Jim said. 'We can't get lost. There's only one way out. We just keep following the passage.'

He inched his way forward, through the splashing stream. Bonnie did indeed cling close, but even though she felt him, she couldn't see him. The water beneath her feet turned to squelching mud. 'We must be in that big cave now,' Jim said, and then, 'I think I've found our tunnel. You'll have to bend down.'

She felt him drop. She felt his heels ahead of her, as she bent down as well. She smelt the dank, soft mud beneath her hands and knees.

'Oh, Jim! I can't bear it! How do we know if this is the right tunnel? Don't go so fast. Wait for me . . . '

She was crawling through a nightmare, a black, close, awful dream. 'It's black like Grandbag's coat,' she thought, ridiculously. 'That's what it's like. And we'll never get out of here, we'll never get out. We'll crawl round here for ever, till we die.'

Suddenly she realized she could see something. What was it? She blinked and stared. It was Jim's heel, right in front of her face. It moved away. She followed it. She could see dim, gleaming walls as well.

'You've found another torch,' Jim said, relief ringing in his voice.

'No, I haven't,' she replied.

With difficulty, Jim turned his head. She could see his streaked, dirty face. She could see his muddy hair. 'What's that underneath your waterproof?'

'What?'

'Something's glowing underneath your waterproof.'

She looked down at herself. He was right. She rolled onto her side and unzipped the waterproof. Godda's necklace gently fell out. It didn't sting her. It didn't hurt. It just glowed in the darkness like a chandelier and the whole tunnel burned softly.

'We can see again, we can see!' Jim cried.

Bonnie gazed at the jewels, amazed. She thought of the angels' hands that had softened her fall.

'Edric and Godda,' she whispered. She looked around her. She saw colours in the rocks that the torch beam could never have shown. Reds and yellows and pinks encrusted on the walls amongst flowing lines of grey.

'Look, Bonnie, look,' said Jim, pointing at silver rivulets that had cut paths in the coloured rocks. 'It's lovely, Bonnie!'

'Yes,' said Bonnie. It was as Arabella had said. There *was* another world beneath the hill. They *did* only know the half. She couldn't find the words for it. 'I'm still cold,' she said instead. 'I'd still give anything to see the sky.'

Jim laughed at her. She wondered if these deep passageways had ever heard laughter before. 'Yes, of course,' he said. 'It *is* cold. Come on then.'

He started crawling again. After a few minutes, the tunnel roof shot up again and they were able to walk side by side. The cave roof above them was streaked with yet more colours. Everything seemed so different.

'This isn't the way we came,' said Bonnie.

'It's just the light,' said Jim. 'It changes things.'

'But we were on our hands and knees,' said Bonnie.

'Right from Batholes. We didn't walk until we got into the big cave.'

'Of course it's the way we came,' said Jim. 'Where else was there for us to go?'

They kept on walking and heard more water ahead of them. The passage bent sharply. They followed it round, and a shower of fine spray burst out of the rock in front of them, a rainbow of fine colours surprised in the soft light of the necklace. Jim stopped and looked at it, puzzled.

'We didn't pass that,' Bonnie said emphatically.

'No,' said Jim. 'We didn't.'

'We're lost.'

'Yes. You're right. I'm sorry, Bonnie. We'll have to go back.'

Bonnie felt sick again. The spectacle of the rainbow spray failed to comfort her. What if they were lost for ever under the hill? What if . . . ?

'There's something here,' said Jim. 'Look.'

She followed his gaze. Halfway up the rocky wall, clear in the necklace-light, was a hole. Beyond it they could hear the gurgling of an underground spring. Jim began to climb.

'Jim, don't go up there!'

'If there's a spring, it may come out somewhere.'

He hauled himself through the hole and out of sight. Bonnie heard him shout, and then she heard a splash, and then nothing.

'Jim, Jim!' She clambered up to the hole. Suddenly, Jim's head appeared. It was washed clean and he was shaking with the cold and grinning. 'We've found a well!'

'What?'

'I'm in a well,' he said. 'It's made of bricks and it's got rungs up the side. I can't see the top, but we can climb up. Come on.'

'Oh, Jim . . . '

His head disappeared. She squeezed through the hole after him. The necklace illuminated a dark pool beneath her and small red bricks and Jim's disappearing body up above. She followed him. They climbed steadily, but there was no light from the world above them. Suddenly, Jim stopped.

'What is it?' Bonnie called.

'I can't go on.'

'Why not?'

'We must be at the top. There's some sort of cover and I can't move the wretched thing.'

It was too cruel. The outside world, the hills, the open sky, could be just feet away. 'We *must* get out,' Bonnie cried, and Jim tried again. 'Shout,' Bonnie said. 'Someone might hear us.'

Jim didn't shout. Quietly, he bowed his head and set his shoulder against what, for all he knew, could have been the whole weight of the hill. He heaved. The cover moved. They saw a starlit shaving of sky before it was all too much, and he let it down again.

'Jim, Jim, you've done it! *Come on . . .* '

He shoved again. The cover trembled. Then it flew skyward in one great burst, which took him by surprise and sent him shooting after it. It fell onto the ground and Jim fell on top of it. Bright light flooded down upon Bonnie. A circle that seemed as wide as the world itself shone above her. It was the circle of the sky.

29

Jim got to his feet. He was in the orchard. The clouds had gone away and so — just — had the night. A new, clear morning struggled for life between the branches of each tree and the cold was fearsome. He leaned down into the well and offered his hand. With his help, Bonnie scrambled out.

In the early morning light, the world was sweet, despite the cold. Bonnie looked with new understanding at the crisp grass beneath her feet. How many times had she run up and down the orchard and never known about the tunnels underneath, the streams, the water-falls, the rainbow sprays, white moths . . . ? She peered between the trees, at the valley. What did she know of the world beyond that now-familiar view of opposite hills? What other valleys, other farmhouses, cities, teeming streets, busy millions lived out there? And up in the sky, beyond the planets and the stars, beyond even the world she'd come from, what lay up there?

'You look blue,' Jim said. 'I think you'd better get back indoors as quick as possible, and change your clothes. I think you oughtn't just to stand there.'

She broke off dreaming, looked at him. He was blue too. His teeth chattered and he squelched every time he moved. She managed a shaky smile. 'The price of being human, hey Jim?'

He didn't smile back. His eye had caught the edge of the holly grove, up the meadow. She looked too. Knew what went through his mind. 'You don't have to go with me,' she said. 'I've been thinking. You could stay, you know. It wasn't your coming that brought Grandmother Marvell here. It was mine. You *should* stay, you know. Think how poor Mrs Onions will feel if you go. And when Arabella comes back and finds I'm gone, she's going to be very lonely. I'd feel so much better if she still had a friend.'

He looked hard at her. 'I mean it,' she said. 'All you have to do is help to launch me. I'd be all right then, wouldn't I?'

'It's the sun and smoke that flies you, not me.' He gestured helplessly. 'You couldn't get off the ground without me, but once you're up . . . '

Once she was up. The thought of soaring up through the sky again made something within Bonnie, despite her distress, tingle with excitement. She too looked up through the orchard towards the holly grove. If she had to go, she wanted to go now, while she felt able to do it. She wanted to go before she had to explain to Mum where Arabella had gone.

'Let's go and light the firepit,' she said. 'We ought to get the balloon out of the barn before everyone gets up.'

'We can't do it now,' he said. 'It's a night job, filling a balloon like that. It'll take hours. We'll do it tonight, if the wind stays down. We'll just have to hope for another clear, bright dawn to launch it. I *will* stay, Bonnie.'

'It would make it so much easier for me to leave them.'

'You're sure?'

'I'm absolutely sure.'

He nodded. It would have been unthinkable once, but he had a choice. He was a real boy and he made his choice freely.

'Oh, thank you, Jim,' Bonnie hugged him and they both squelched, clammy with mud.

'You ought to go indoors and change, you know,' he said again. 'You do look dreadful. If you stay like that you'll make yourself ill and then you won't be well enough to go at all.'

Together they hauled the cover back over the well, and piled on the few stones that Jim had knocked over in his flight. Then Jim said he'd see her later. Bonnie watched him squelch up through the orchard, before turning, herself, back to the house.

'If Dad finds out I've been on the hill again, I don't know what he'll do,' she chattered through her teeth. 'Let's hope no one's awake yet. Let's hope I can get back in without him seeing me. What am I going to tell Mum about Arabella?'

In the scullery, she peeled out of her waterproofs and hid them behind the log pile, and surveyed the cold, damp mess which the rest of her clothes had become. Listening at the kitchen door, she heard no sound of life, so she opened it cautiously and tiptoed in. The kitchen was empty. The clock ticked half-past seven. She felt as if she'd been gone, not hours but days. She removed her soggy socks and dried her feet and crept past the cats, up the stairs.

Mum was dressing Florence. The door was ajar and she could hear Florence's baby talk as she tiptoed past. She shut herself in the bathroom. *What was she going to say about Arabella*? Her brain was frozen. Her whole being was one lump of pain. She filled up the big white bath and climbed into it and melted the pain away. When she could think again, felt human again, she dried herself and wrapped the towel round her and returned to the bedroom to contemplate the problem properly.

'Oh, there you are,' said Arabella. 'I was beginning to think you'd gone somewhere. I was getting worried.'

Bonnie's new-found warmth drained away. Arabella sat on her bed, brushing her hair. The bed was made. She was dressed.

'But you . . . I mean . . . ' Bonnie pointed weakly at the wardrobe. 'I . . . I thought . . . '

Briefly, Arabella stopped brushing. For a flicker of a moment, empty, dull eyes, like the Jake-thing's eyes, searched Bonnie's face. Then she was brushing again and a flurry of uncharacteristic chatter poured out of her.

'I'll just finish my hair. There. It's done. I'll go and see if Mum and Dad are up. I'm hungry. I'll open out the stove and start the breakfast. Have you noticed, the fog's gone? Mum says we won't do any more lessons till after Christmas now. Did I tell you . . . '

'You're not Arabella!' Bonnie said.

The chatter stopped.

'You're not Arabella.'

'Have you thought about Christmas presents?' The chatter started again, as if she hadn't said it. 'You know, it's really time. I'd like to make sweets for everyone. I thought I'd wrap them in silver foil and make a pretty box for them. We could do it today, if we haven't got any lessons.'

Bonnie sank down òn her own bed. The words went on and on. Her eyes lifted above the girl's head, out of the window to the path where Jim had gone. How long she sat like that, she didn't know. Nor did she know what she thought all that time. The Arabella-thing got up and touched her and she nearly jumped out of her skin.

'Aren't you coming down for breakfast?'

'Oh. Yes.'

Bonnie flung on some clean clothes and they both made their way downstairs, past the portraits of the ancestors. Did they know, Bonnie wondered, what walked past them? Did they care?

Dad was eating breakfast. Florence was playing with the cats. Mum looked up as the girls came in, and the Arabella-thing began chattering again.

'I'm almost glad that this time tomorrow I'll be gone,' Bonnie thought. 'It's going to be a long hard day . . . '

Mum asked her to pick up Florence and put her in her

chair and give her breakfast. She thought, 'This is the last time she'll ever ask me to do that . . . '

And so it continued all day, and it *was* a long hard day. She ate the last lunch, watched the last afternoon shadows on the wall, lit the fire in the inglenook for the last time, saw the last sunset. And, through it all, the Arabella-thing chattered incessantly and Bonnie realized that if she stopped, her emptiness — the way things really were — would be plain to see.

After tea, Mum departed, weary as ever, to do what she described as 'things for Christmas' in her sewing-room. Dad drew himself and his account book close to the fire and said he still had some catching up to do. The Arabella-thing announced her intention of going to bed. She looked exhausted. She couldn't keep up the chatter any more.

When she'd gone, Bonnie strode about restlessly. Eventually, she said perhaps she'd go up too. She couldn't bear the last chiming of nine o'clock, the last embers on the last fire, the last sight of Dad's head bowed over his books . . .

'All right,' said Dad. 'Good night. You probably need to go to bed early after last night's nonsense . . . '

'How little he knows of last night's nonsense,' Bonnie thought and, if she hadn't been so sad, she'd have smiled. She lingered in the doorway. Despite herself, she drank in the end of her very last day.

'What is it?' Dad said.

'Oh, nothing.'

Instead of going through the kitchen and up the stairs, she went out into the hall. Something drew her to Mum's sewing-room door. She stood outside it and then, realizing that she didn't know what she was doing there, turned away and began to climb the hall stairs.

'Are you off to bed? It's very early.'

A patch of light was thrown across the hall. Mum stood in her doorway.

'I'm tired,' Bonnie said, and it was true. She was tired of pretending, tired of smiling, tired of the pain inside her. She saw beyond Mum into the sewing-room, saw the thick, velvet curtains. She caught a glimpse of packages and wrapping-paper. Mum pulled the door behind her, to keep her secrets hidden. They stood now in semi-darkness. Mum's face was tired too.

'I . . . I feel I've let you down,' she said.

'I don't know what you mean.'

'I think you do. Something's wrong, isn't it? I'd have known what it was once . . . Oh, I know I'll be myself again when the baby's born, but I hate being like this. What's the matter with Arabella?'

'A . . . Arabella's tired too,' Bonnie blustered awkwardly. 'That's all. We stay up talking till late. She's never had a friend before. There's really nothing wrong.'

It sounded lame, and they both knew it. 'Do you mean I'm worrying about nothing?' Mum said, as if she didn't think she was.

Bonnie thought about spilling it all out, and knew she couldn't. 'That's right,' she said instead. 'You mustn't worry about things. You've got to take things nice and easy.'

Mum sighed. 'It's all right. You don't have to tell me if you don't want to. You surely know by now that I never pry.'

Bonnie tried to protest and Mum changed the subject. 'Did you know, there's going to be a storm?' she said. 'You wouldn't think so, would you? It seems so calm. Dad says it'll snow in the next day or so . . . We've got skis somewhere in the scullery. We'll have to teach you how to use them.'

Bonnie felt wretched. 'I like the snow,' was all that she could manage as Mum turned back to her sewing-room. She felt herself weakening, changing her mind. She *was* going to burden Mum with the whole, awful truth . . .

'Good night,' said Mum. She shut the sewing-room

n the bedroom, the Arabella-thing was breathing deeply. Bonnie got into bed. She couldn't sleep. She got out again, looked out of the window, up the hill. There was no fire yet. It wasn't time. She got her cardboard suitcase out from beneath the bed and opened her drawer quietly and plucked out the few clothes that were really hers. She tossed them miserably into the case, and got back into bed. Mum's clock next door struck ten. Still she was awake. It struck eleven. She tossed and turned, as he tried not to remember all the good things Highholly Hill had brought her. It struck twelve. Had ever a midnight, ever a dark tunnel out of Batholes, ever Grandbag's coat or a night sky even, been as black as this? At last, exhausted, she fell asleep.

When Bonnie awoke again, there was light up on the hill. She saw it straight away, saw a red smudge between he dark hollies. She sat up. It was no dream. It was really here and the sky was midnight blue, like the balloon, nd morning was on the way.

She got out of bed. Her toe stubbed against the cardboard suitcase. Tears of anger sprang from her eyes. Now hat it had come to it, she *couldn't* go.

'There *has* to be another way,' she said out loud. There *has* to be another way. I won't go. I won't.'

She strode up and down, and the Arabella-thing tirred. Briefly her eyes opened and Bonnie stopped nd looked at her. It was as if she was empty, as if othing was there. Her tongue fell out of her mouth as if there was no active mind at home to keep it in. A silver dribble rolled down her chin.

'Oh, Arabella, Arabella, Arabella . . . '

Bonnie looked above her, through the window, up into the moody blue sky. Suddenly it seemed as if this was the moment that everything in her life — all those years of dreaming of a land beyond the sky, all the things she'd done since she came here — had been pointing to. As if this was what she came here for. Not to jump heroically out of a window, or to look for Wild Edric in a thunderstorm, or to save them all by finding him under the ground — but to perform this boring, quiet, ridiculous act of self-sacrifice. She almost laughed out loud. So it was her lot in life to go back to chip papers and orange neon lights out on the street, Maybelle crying when things didn't go her way, and Grandbag . . .

'If you can beat her here, you can beat her there as well,' she said to herself.

'Can I?' she answered.

'You know you can . . .'

She dressed quickly and looked at herself for the last time in the dressing-table mirror. Godda's necklace glittered at her, and she touched it.

'At least I've got you,' she whispered. 'I've got *some-thing* that'll prove it really happened, when I get home. A real treasure of my own. Not, of course, that I'd ever sell you. I'd never do that, or give you to a museum. It'll just be nice to *have* you. Like owning a famous painting. I've never had anything like that before. Most people never do.'

Picking up the suitcase, she left the bedroom without another glance at Arabella and passed the other bedrooms carefully. She was good at creeping now. She knew which floorboards to avoid, which doors creaked, which stairs had to be stepped over. She came down into the kitchen. The Jake-thing lay still as death. He too was dribbling, and Bonnie longed for the real Jake to bound out onto the hill with her, the way he used to do. The cream cats were all awake. They watched her with round, yellow eyes. When she lifted the latch they came and rubbed themselves against her legs and miaowed as though saying 'won't we do instead?' and slid out into the scullery ahead of her.

'Goodbye,' she said to the kitchen, but only the kettle on the stove hissed back at her. She passed through the scullery, out into a still frost. The cream cats waited for her.

'What is it?' she said. 'Why don't you go away?'

They were a reminder of Michael, a first step on the long journey home. Bonnie remembered the flint-faced house with its mushroom shaped roof. She remembered the verandah and Michael's cats. She remembered the thick smoke as it filled the tottering, monstrous balloon, and the flickering shape of what Jim used to be, as he struggled with Michael to straighten the thing, control it, hold it down as it filled to capacity, as it reached for the sky . . .

'You're off, are you?'

Someone moved in the shadow of the house. Someone with still, grey eyes that glistened in the dark . . .

'Dad!'

He leaned against a wall which glittered with frost. She dropped the suitcase. She couldn't move. 'Dad, oh Dad . . .'

'We wouldn't let you go without saying goodbye,' he said. His words made great, white clouds of breath. She stepped towards him, but her weak knees actually began to sink. He took her hands as he saw her going down, and held her tightly.

'How did you know?' she said.

He laughed. 'Oh, I don't know the half of it,' he said. I don't know what it's all *really* about. But I do know how you got here. I've smelt the smoke on that blue balloon of yours, and seen the soot inside. I know you came with

Jim too. I'm not a fool. And I've seen those pits up in the holly grove, and the logs and staves. I've seen your face, Bonnie, when you didn't know anyone was looking. I watched you tonight, striding up and down . . .'

'Oh, Dad . . .' Bonnie hung her head. She'd thought — Arabella had thought — that they couldn't tell him things, that they'd have to go to Mum or nobody at all. It was they who'd been fools.

'Enough of this,' Dad said. He picked up the suitcase. 'Come on. Let's go. Jim got the balloon out of the barn hours ago. We've got it nearly full. There's something very strange about the way that boy can move. I left him at it, said I'd come down and get you.'

For the first time, Bonnie smelt the soot on Dad, saw his dusty coat and smoke-streaked face. He'd helped to get the balloon up. He'd been out all night.

'Mum said this wasn't a place like anywhere else I'd been,' Bonnie said. 'She was right, but I'm still not sure that I know what kind of place it is.'

Dad laughed. 'I don't think any of us knows what kind of place this is,' he said. 'Sometimes it seems just like anywhere. Sometimes it's quite, quite different from the rest of the world.' He squeezed her hand. The sky was lightening. 'Come on,' he said again and he led her along the terrace, through the orchard, up into the meadow where, ahead of them, the great shape of the balloon towered above the circle of the holly trees.

'If there was a land beyond the sky, would you be surprised?' Bonnie said.

Dad looked from the balloon to the stars in the dark blue up above him. 'I wouldn't be surprised at *anything*,' he said.

'When I've gone . . .'

'Don't worry. I'll tell Mum you said goodbye. I'll tell her you're all right.'

The grass crunched beneath Bonnie's feet. Her breath made great white clouds. She climbed and didn't speak again. As they came to the holly grove, the roaring of the great fire reached out to them. Bonnie stood with a cold, white world on one side of her and a furious red one on the other. In the red one, Jim dashed back and forth and there was indeed something very strange about the way he moved. This was the last vestige, she supposed, of his being a shadowboy. He looked like twenty men. He looked as if he was everywhere. He'd got the balloon tethered and staved. He'd got its mouth over the smoke pit. The smoke was filling it and his hands, which seemed to reach every side of it, all at the same time, struggled to hold it down.

'Here, let me help you,' Dad called. He dropped the suitcase and pushed through the trees and Bonnie was left alone between the worlds. She watched their silhouettes as they struggled. Her face felt the heat. Flakes of ash filled the air. She smelt something. What was it? Something *beyond* the smell of fire. Flakes rained down around her and she remembered that other night when she'd run away from home.

The smell beyond the fire was the smell of home.

It was like the end of the holiday, when you remember where you come from. Bonnie remembered Maybelle. Really remembered her. She remembered the red-and-yellow bedroom and the floppy plant and her raggedy doll that she'd never left behind before. And she wanted Maybelle. She wanted the long-promised home that they'd begun to make together. She picked up the cardboard suitcase, clutched it in her arms, lovingly, surprised. This couldn't be her, could it, feeling this way? She looked for the last time upon the back of the house, the valley, the hills beyond which the sun was lightening the sky.

'Come and help us, will you, Bonnie?' Dad called.

As she ducked under the hollies, the necklace slithered off her neck. It fell onto the earth, its silver hands unclasped again. She stopped and stared. Godda's blue enamel substitute for sky, her diamond stars, lay at her feet. She picked it up and held it in her hand. She was going to be like the ordinary people after all, who never had a treasure of their own. She should have been sad. She would have cried once at life's unfairness.

'It's *really* over,' was all that she could say and her eyes drank in every bit of it, so that she'd always remember.

'Bonnie,' Jim called. 'It's nearly time for you to go. Come on . . .'

She hung the necklace in the nearest holly tree, struggled through the growing dawn into a fierce world where everything roared and flickered and there were no pale contours any more. The balloon was full and raging to be away. Dad and what seemed like a dozen spinning Jims had pegged it down and it bobbed impatiently. They struggled with the gondola and Jim shouted at her to damp down the fire, which she did, and step with them underneath the great, greedy mouth.

'It's time,' he said, when she got close. His body stilled to that of one panting, ordinary boy who'd never do a thing like this again, whose last connection with the old life tore at its tethers to get free of him. 'Take my hand. I'll tie you in.' He threw her suitcase into the gondola. Handed her in after it. Began to tie her down.

'Sun's nearly up,' Dad shouted. 'Look at the sky!'

Bonnie's heart began to pound. She gripped the sides of the gondola. The air was perfectly still. Above her the sky was pink and between the hollies she could see it turning to gold. Dad followed Jim and began untethering. The gondola lurched and shook. Jim cut the last ropes and the staves crashed down. Dad didn't say goodbye. He didn't reach out and touch Bonnie, and she was glad. He stood with his arms folded and his face lifted and his still, steady eyes watching her go. Jim raised a hand.

Bonnie felt Highholly Hill falling away. First the holly grove. Then Highholly House. Then the sheep's path to the top and Batholes and Edric's Throne and Roundhill and the cottages down at the back. She saw a light in Arabella's bedroom. Saw a figure open the window to look out. She clutched the gondola. It was . . . it was . . .

The thinnest veil of cloud hid her view. She struggled to see. It couldn't have been the drooling, awful Arabella-thing. Not with a hand raised up triumphantly like that. She came through the cloud and was shocked that she couldn't find Highholly Hill among the other valleys and hills. She strained her eyes, found, at last, its white stones on the top and thought of Edric and Godda.

'That *was* Arabella, wasn't it?' she said out loud. 'She has come back, hasn't she? Everything *is* all right . . . ?'

Like an answer, the sun appeared. The cloud was torn away and Bonnie could see it beyond the rim of the earth. 'Oh God, oh God in heaven,' she breathed, '*I can see the Earth's curve!*'

Then, unexpectedly, she heard music. Sweet pipe music that she'd forgotten about. The music of the skies. It mingled with the last of the stars and she knew Arabella was back home. Everything *was* all right. Above her she could see the balloon, the richest, darkest blue now in the sunlight, and the planets above them both and summertime right round the other side of the earth below. The sky above her parted. It opened for her and let her through and for a moment the brightness of it was so great that she couldn't see at all, and then she found that she was falling, that the music was gone, that the bright-ness had faded and the faintest breeze stirred the gon-dola, as though a change of weather was on the way. The faintest murmur of a different world rose up to greet her.

She dropped through an ordinary, early-morning sky into grey clouds. The gondola shook again and the cold bit at her cheeks. She stared and stared and wondered what lay down there. Then she smelt something. What was it? It came from below. It was a strange, flat, grubby smell that she couldn't identify. Something familiar . . .

31

The balloon slipped immaculately between power lines and telephone wires. Only at the last minute did Bonnie recognize the flats and the tarmac forecourt and the holly trees and Michael's garden and the clearing in the middle of it. The trees round the edge of the clearing reached up strong, bony fingers and the balloon became entangled in them. Bonnie was jerked hard. The gondola swung precariously, ten feet above the ground. The branches snapped, and Bonnie and the gondola came down. They were both flung onto their side. The monster that had carried them came to its end. It hung, torn, among the branches, a wrinkled bag of dull, dark cloth again.

Bonnie struggled with the knots that tied her in. Everything around her was very still and the traffic sounded far away. She rubbed her sore bones and looked up at Michael's house. The curtains were tightly drawn. There were no cats on the verandah. The summer chairs and tables were gone and the verandah was bare. As Bonnie untied the last knots, she remembered saying, 'It'll be like stories in books, when people return to find they were only gone for a moment in time . . . ' She looked around her. The ground was covered with fallen, rotting leaves. Between the bare branches of the trees, she saw the garden wall. She'd got it wrong, hadn't she? It was winter here too. What would she tell Maybelle, who lived beyond that wall?

Slowly, she got up. She turned away from the flint-faced house and Michael, who she'd see later. She began woodenly to make her way between the trees. The world was dull and grey and cold. A flake or two of snow began to fall. She found the hole in the wall and clambered through. How could she make Maybelle believe her, she asked herself, as she pushed between the prickly hollies on the other side. She reached the tarmac fore-court. Beyond the flats she could see traffic lights change colour on the road, and a row of tinsel-decorated shops, ready for Christmas but still closed, because it was still early or maybe even Sunday. She saw empty pavements and milk crates piled up in front of the flats, waiting for the milkman to collect them, and stray dogs around the dustbins by the orange wall. She saw the sign by the road which said HIGHHOLLY HOUSE Nos. 1-79. It had been drawn all over. It was hard to read the words. She looked beyond the sign, at the flats themselves. Numbers 1-79 . . . Which dark entrance hole was hers? She couldn't remember. They all looked the same.

Then she saw the fire escape and her balcony and the entrance underneath it. She remembered Grandbag's car, parked just there. Of course. She crossed the fore-court. Made for the stairs. They were dark and smelly as she came in out of the snow. Huge, rude words were scrawled in fantastic colours up the wall. Bonnie climbed past them to the first floor and began to make her way along the walkway, reading the numbers on the doors.

At last she stood outside her own front door. Her heart beat very fast. She looked over the balcony rail. Down in the courtyard she saw a mass of washing-lines and a solitary bare tree. Quiet snowflakes were falling out of what was now a nasty, yellow sky. She turned back to the door. It sounded very quiet inside. She rang the shrill bell hard because she knew that, if Maybelle didn't hear, her courage would fail and she'd run away again.

Someone moved. Through the little bit of frosted glass she saw a light go on and then a shape coming down the hall. She heard footsteps. The door opened.

Someone stood there, and at first Bonnie thought it was Grandbag.

'Well, well, well . . . ' the someone said, in Grandbag's voice.

'D . . . Doreen . . . !' Bonnie said. 'Doreen, is that you?'

Doreen folded her arms. The most unwelcoming smile lit her eyes. Her thin shoulders were covered in the sort of fancy dressing-gown that Grandbag always used to wear. Bonnie remembered Doreen's shapeless, ugly dresses and her nervousness. Whatever had happened?

'Yes, it's me,' Doreen said. 'So you're back. You'd better come in. It's cold with the door open. I'm useless till I've had a cup of tea.'

'Where's Maybelle?' Bonnie said, uncertainly.

Doreen didn't answer. She tottered down the hall to the kitchen. Not sure if she was doing the right thing, Bonnie shut the front door and followed her. When she entered the kitchen, she couldn't believe her eyes. Everything was as different as it could be. The room had that cluttered look she associated with Grandbag. Her legs went weak at the sight of it. She moved a pile of newspapers off a chair and sank onto it. There were no pretty, fanciful, silly things. No signs of Maybelle anywhere.

Doreen made the tea. She stood by the kettle with arms folded while Bonnie looked around. What had happened? She didn't seem like Doreen any more. Perhaps it was just the dressing-gown. She poured the tea, just for herself, and drank a cup of it and said at last, accusingly, 'Where've you been, then?'

'I . . . I'd rather tell Maybelle, if you don't mind,' Bonnie answered resolutely.

Doreen's eyes glimmered. 'You'll have a long wait then,' came her tart reply.

'You mean . . . ?'

'They've had a row,' Doreen said. 'She's gone. She said some nasty things. Mother'll never be the same again. You mustn't mention her to Mother. I'll wake her and tell her you're here. I'll take you in to see her, but you mustn't tire her. She's not what she was, you know.' She emptied the teapot into another cup. 'I have to do *everything* now,' she said, and marched off with the tea.

Bonnie's dread of seeing Grandbag again, even her anxiety about finding Maybelle, became quite swallowed up in curiosity. Why was Doreen so different? Where was the meek, nervous Doreen now? It was as if the world had turned upside down.

Doreen reappeared. 'Come on,' she said. 'I've woken her up specially.'

She hustled Bonnie down the rest of the hall to what had been the door of her own room. She opened it and pushed her in.

'Here she is, Mother,' she shouted. 'Don't talk to her too long. You'll tire yourself. I'll go and get your breakfast. Don't try and get up. You know it's not good for you.'

The room was desperately stuffy, with the window closed and the curtains almost completely drawn and a little side-lamp by the bed that illuminated the dust. Grandbag lay in bed. The black dye had come out of her hair and she wore no make-up. She looked about a hundred years old. She lay back on the pillows. Her nightdress was grubby. She looked so small. The cocky, triumphant look was out of her eyes, but the bitterness was still there. Bitterness and anger.

'Well, you're back,' she said.

'Yes, Grandma.'

'Good. You can make sure that fool of a woman stops feeding me brown bread. I hate brown bread. She does it just to annoy me. You can bring me the newspapers. I hear them drop through the letterbox every day, but she never lets me have them.'

'Where's my mother?'

'Your what?'

'I want to know where my mother is.'

Grandbag stared. 'Your mother?'

'I'm talking about Maybelle,' Bonnie said determinedly.

'Such a pretty name,' Grandbag said. 'I used to know a girl called Maybelle . . . ' She peered at Bonnie cautiously. 'Do I know you?'

'I'm Bonnie,' Bonnie said. 'You know I am. Look, Grandma, it's me.'

Grandbag began to struggle up in the bed, but she couldn't do it. She clawed unsuccessfully at the covers, and fell back down again. 'It used to be so different,' she muttered to herself as if the effort was all too much for her and she'd forgotten Bonnie was there. 'I didn't used to be like this at all.'

'Grandma,' Bonnie said, moving round the bed, so Grandbag could see her again. 'What's happened? You've never been like this before. And what's happened to Doreen? I don't understand.'

'She treats me terrible now,' Grandbag said. 'She knows I'm too weak to pay her back. I know what she's doing. She's getting her revenge.'

'But Maybelle . . . '

'We had a row, Maybelle and I. After all the years of things I've done for her. After looking after that child for her. After all my care. She said terrible things. I don't know where she got them from. Terrible things they were. I can't forget them. I dream about them at night. They make me shake when I think about them . . . '

'*And they're all true, aren't they, Mother?*'

Doreen stood in the doorway, gloating. 'You know it, Mother. Every word she said was true. That's why it makes you so ill to think of it. I've got your breakfast ready. Come on. Sit up. Here you are. Brown bread and butter.'

Bonnie pushed past Doreen and ran down the hall.

'What do you think you're doing now?' Doreen called.

Bonnie struggled with the front door. She stumbled outside. It was snowing hard now, but the cold air was wonderful. It was full of city smells and noises, but it was fresh and true and she gulped it in. The stale breath inside that flat was the very air of hate.

'There she goes. Off again,' said Doreen. 'Isn't that a shame?' She didn't run after Bonnie. She shut Grandbag back into her airless room again, and closed the front door. She stood in front of the hall mirror and stared long at her changed face.

Bonnie clattered down the stairs and sank in a heap on the last of them. So that was her home. That was what she'd come back to. Oh, that awful, airless room didn't bear any resemblance to the singing, lively, red-and-yellow room she and Maybelle had painted. And where *was* Maybelle? Would she ever find her? She stared out at the thickening snowstorm and began to cry, covering her face with her hands.

'It's all right,' a voice said. 'It's not as bad as it seems. Honestly. Come and have some breakfast with me.'

She looked up. It was Michael.

32

Michael brought Bonnie toast and coffee on a tray. She sat in front of his paraffin heater, surrounded by shelves and books and bits and pieces, and remembered that other morning when he'd given her breakfast. It all now seemed so long ago. It had been the day he'd told her about the land beyond the sky.

'You still have the flying book?' she said.

'Of course I do.'

He got it down and thumbed through the yellow-edged pages till he found the right one. She peered where he pointed, at the broken pottery with its balloon-and-fire decorations that no longer held any mystery.

'Maybe you'll write your own story, one day,' he said.

'Nobody'll believe it really happened, though.' She shut the book. 'Do you know, my aunt Doreen is just terrible now. She's terrifying. She's just like Grandbag used to be and Grandbag's . . . '

'Grandbag's had it.'

'That's right. How did you know that?'

'It's what Maybelle said. It stuck in my mind.'

'Maybelle? You've seen her then? You know where she is?'

'Oh yes,' Michael said. 'She came to see me before she left. They'd had a big row, she and her mother. She thought she'd never see you again, you see. She blamed her mother for driving you away. She said, "I shouted at her. I told her the truth. It's what I should have done long ago. She crumpled, you know. I think she's had it. She'll never be the same again." She said her sister Doreen had all the malice of a liberated prisoner towards her former jailer . . . '

But Bonnie didn't care about Doreen any more, or Grandbag, who was just something from the past, now that Maybelle — brave at last — had dealt with her. 'Where *is* Maybelle?' she said. She looked around impatiently, as if she expected her to spring out of a cupboard.

Michael laughed. 'She's not in here,' he said. 'Finish your breakfast and I'll take you to her. We'll make up a thermos flask of coffee and it might be a good idea to take hot water bottles. The heater in my old car's not much good.'

But Bonnie couldn't finish her breakfast. 'Does she know where I've been?'

'I told her,' Michael said. 'I showed her the book and promised I'd let her know the moment you returned. I don't know why, but in the end I think she half-seemed to believe me. Maybe it sounded a bit more hopeful than the police saying you were just another runaway child and they'd done everything they could. I go to see her sometimes. Just to make sure she doesn't think I've forgotten. She comes up here too, just in case I'm mad and I've got it all wrong, to look for you. But I think she does almost believe I'm some sort of link with you.'

As he spoke, he drew back the curtains. In the world outside, demented snowflakes hurtled everywhere. 'We are in for a bit of a bad journey,' he said. 'But I don't mind if you don't, though we ought to be prepared for the worst.' He began gathering together scarves and gloves and hats. He found pairs of wellington boots. 'Pass me those blankets, will you?'

A couple of tartan travel rugs were draped over a large crate. Bonnie picked them up. 'What's this?' she said, looking into the crate.

Michael glanced over. 'It's my telescope.'

Bonnie remembered Michael's perfect observatory above, with its glass dome pushing up into the sky. 'But Michael, why . . .'

He stopped his busy rushing and looked at her. 'It's turned out all right and you're back again,' he said. 'But I never should have let you get involved. I must have been mad. Your mother was beside herself, you know. I swore I'd never look into the sky again.'

Bonnie touched the telescope. 'You must set it up again,' she said. 'I was meant to go. It was really *nothing* to do with you. I'll tell you all about it, later, when we get to Maybelle.'

Thick snow blocked two lanes of the motorway. More of the stuff tipped out of the dark sky and the wind blew it this way and that like powdery sand dunes at the edge of the sea. The motorway signs warned that 30 miles an hour was the maximum speed that anyone should do, but the long convoy of traffic limped much slower than that.

Michael had been right about the heater in his car. It didn't work. As they crawled over cities and out again and through the countryside, between white flanks of fields, Bonnie began to freeze. They stopped at a motorway service station and drank soup and refilled hot water bottles. Then Bonnie climbed back into the car and entwined herself in travel rugs again and clutched the hot water bottles tight. Michael steered a course back onto the motorway.

'It wouldn't take long now, on a good day,' he said. They drove past huge cooling towers and a ruined factory with hundreds of broken windows. The snow was still tipping down. It was hard to see at all. 'Goodness knows how long we'll take in this.'

Bonnie didn't hear him. She didn't see them reach the countryside again. An awful thought had crept out of her mind. What if Maybelle, like Doreen, had all the malice of a liberated prisoner? What if freedom had made *her* bitter and cruel? What if the Maybelle they crawled towards through the blizzard wasn't the one she remembered, the one she wanted her to be?'

'This is our junction,' Michael said.

They slipped off the motorway. The road sign, half covered in snow, told them it was twenty miles to the nearest town. The road was completely empty. Bonnie looked around her. They were driving into an almost alpine landscape of valleys and hills and the sky was lightening and the falling snow was beginning to thin.

'Where are we, Michael?'

He didn't answer her. He hunched over the wheel as if frozen to it, and peered through the gap that the wobbling windscreen wipers made.

'Where are we going?' she said.

'It's special where your mother is,' he said simply. 'Just wait and see.'

He turned the car off the main road. They drove through snowbound villages, between cascading, sculpted banks of the stuff. A snow-plough passed them on the other side of the road, with its lights flashing. It was the first vehicle they'd seen. They drove through a deserted town, then out the other side, down a hill, then up the other side again. They came over the top of the hill. A whole new valley opened out in front of them. The snow had almost stopped. In the distance, against the brighter sky, Bonnie saw the silhouette of a high hill with lumps of rock on top of it.

'Is something wrong?' Michael said. 'You're not feeling sick, are you? It's been a long journey. We'll stop and have another drink, shall we?'

He pulled up the car. Bonnie's face had gone the colour of the sky before the snowstorm hit. He poured out the last of the coffee and coaxed it down her throat.

Bonnie hardly noticed what he did. She stared through the windscreen. The last flakes settled. Watery, pink sunlight struggled in the sky above the distant hill. In the sky above the standing stones. The standing stones, surely, of Highholly Hill . . .

'Don't know what they call them. They're quite a sight, aren't they?' said Michael.

'Yes,' said Bonnie weakly.

'That's where she is,' said Michael. 'You wouldn't believe it, would you? Right up there. Do you think you'll be all right now? We ought to get on. The last bit could be the worst. We could get stuck. We could have to walk and it's three o'clock now and we don't want to do that in the dark.'

'Yes,' said Bonnie weakly again. 'Don't worry about me. I'm all right now.'

He looked at her pale face uncertainly.

'Really,' she said.

He started the engine. 'Do you know,' he said, 'they make a better job of clearing these little roads than they do on the motorway. Funny that, isn't it?' The road was gritted and clear. He drove fast. The pink sky behind Highholly Hill said that the day was ending. The car slithered round a corner and he apologized.

'It's all right,' said Bonnie, still in a dream. The hill was right up above them now. He spun round another corner and the road ahead was straight. They passed a village sign and a warning about tractors crossing. Michael slowed down. Bonnie saw the garage and the road down to the showground and the lane that led up to the bumpy track.

'We're here,' she whispered dreamily. 'We're here.'

Michael looked at her strangely. 'That's right,' he said.

'Up here,' she said.

'How did you know that?'

He turned where she pointed. She didn't answer him. They drove up between cottages. The lane hadn't been cleared. He slowed right down. The car wheels skidded and they came to a halt. A woman outside a house was shovelling snow. He wound down the window.

'You can't go up there,' she said, looking the car up and down. 'Leastways, not in that.'

'I suppose not, but we can't go back,' Michael said. 'We've come a long way.'

'Then you'd best walk,' she replied. 'You won't get lost if you keep inside the lane, between the hedges. Long as it don't snow again.' She looked up at the sky which was darkening, more from the end of day than from the advent of fresh snow. 'Have you boots? Would you like to take the spare shovel?'

They got out of the car. Michael accepted the offer of the shovel and got out their boots.

'She's mad up there, you know,' the woman said as he began to change out of his shoes. 'Up there alone. She'll never stick the winter out . . . '

A sudden burst of fresh wind blew the light snow against the side of the car and up into Bonnie's face. It woke her out of her dream. She looked from the woman to Michael, who didn't understand yet. She wanted to laugh. Why, they'd *all* stick it out. He'd know that soon. She put on the pair of thick socks that Michael offered her, and slipped into his spare boots. She was impatient to get the village behind her, impatient for the hill. She couldn't believe this was happening to her. Couldn't believe it at all.

'Put your gloves on,' Michael said. 'It's a long way. We've got to keep you warm. That's right. And how about this blanket?' He tied one of the travel rugs round her shoulders. 'Not too heavy?'

She shook her head and jumped up and down.

'It won't be as hard as it looks,' Michael said. 'We'll be all right.'

'I know we will,' she said.

They began the climb. At first it wasn't hard at all, despite the big boots and the heavy clothes. As the track wound and the hedges bowed beneath the weight of snow, Bonnie caught glimpses of Highholly House below the brow of the hill, with a light in a window that beckoned to her like an advent star. Her legs began to ache. She pulled them out of the deep snow, one after the other. There was a wonderful stillness everywhere. They both climbed quietly. The only sound was the crunch, crunch, crunch of their feet.

At last they dipped down into the Dingle. The banks rose and the trees thickened on either side. Bonnie heard the brook before they came to it. She stopped at the wooden bridge and leaned against the side and banged her numb hands together. Snow fell from a branch. A bird flew up into the sky. She peered down at the fast flowing water. In the world of memory, two girls had waded through that brook . . .

They climbed out of the Dingle on the other side. The landscape opened out.

'Look at it all,' said Michael. The sky was that magic dark blue again. The moon was up and shining on the snow. There was a glittering, pale-blue sheen over everything. 'It's special, isn't it? Do you know what I mean?'

Bonnie looked at the valley that she knew so well, the twinkling lights, each one in its right place, and the hills she'd last seen from the gondola.

'I know what you mean.'

They climbed on. This was the long, hard bit. It seemed to carry on for ever. The stars were all out now. The light of the house at last was close. Bonnie shivered and gasped for breath. The yard gate loomed ahead of them and suddenly she couldn't, just *couldn't* believe that everything was all right, that something terrible wouldn't happen to spoil it all. 'She *will* be like Doreen. She *will* have changed. She *will* be awful,' she thought.

Michael reached the gate and opened it. They hauled their aching limbs into the yard. It was empty and abandoned. The big barn door was off its hinge. There was no straw inside. No animals any more.

212

'Sad, isn't it?' said Michael. 'It must have been a really good farm once, and now it's not worked at all. Seems such a waste . . . '

Bonnie looked up. The terrace gate had come off. The paint on the scullery door was peeling. An upstairs window-pane, Mum's she thought, was broken and had been covered with polythene.

But it was beautiful, all the same. Beautiful and perfect. She didn't mind its state of disrepair.

Michael squeezed her arm. 'Come on!' He led her through the creaking gate, onto the terrace. 'This is the way.' He led her to the scullery door, which shuddered as it always had done, as he pushed it open. He directed her through the scullery with its smells of logs and dust and mouse. He banged on the kitchen door and lifted the latch.

'In you go.' The kitchen was unlit, but the night was bright and Bonnie saw everything clearly. The kettle on the stove hissed at her, just the same as ever. But there was no fine old table, no dresser, no stocked pantry with its laden shelves, no armchair on the rug by the stove. A row of old plates were set up on a shelf by the stairs' door. Some cups hung from hooks beneath it. A small, red, formica table stood in the middle of the floor with the remains of a single meal on it. A pile of washing-up sat in the sink. On the shelf where Dad's silver cup from the Show had been placed sat Bonnie's raggedy doll.

A dog lay beneath the window. It got to its feet and shook itself all over. Its hair was silky and soft, like Jake's used to be. It didn't bark. Bonnie crossed the floor to look at it. It lifted its head. It was the sort of dog you could imagine galloping across hills.

Someone walked across the living-room next door. Bonnie heard a very distant buzz of radio and the far door being shut. She heard the footsteps coming closer. 'Oh!' she cried out. She couldn't help herself.

'Who is it? Who's there?' Maybelle's voice called, nervously. And Bonnie couldn't speak.

'It's all right, Maybelle,' Michael said.

'Michael . . . ' Her voice softened. She was pleased. The door between the room opened and a yellow square of light was thrown across the floor.

Bonnie stepped forward. She couldn't see the sagging beams any more, or the flagstones, or the stove. All she could see, all that mattered, was the unchanged shape of Maybelle in the doorway. Maybelle with her untidy hair and blobs of make-up and sagging sweater and holey slippers. Maybelle with the teapot dropping between her fingers towards the floor. Maybelle with her face white as death and her eyes staring, round and wild . . .

'Bonnie, dear God, my Bonnie! *My Bonnie!*'

For a moment, neither of them could move. Maybelle stared at Bonnie, wrapped up like a refugee's bundle in her rug, with her head poking out of the top of it and bright tears in her eyes. Then they fell upon each other like fierce wild animals. Maybelle pulled the rug off and held Bonnie tight. She held her head in her hands. She clung to her. She wept into her hair. She kissed her cheeks.

'Bonnie, Bonnie, Bonnie . . . '

'Maybelle, oh Maybelle, I love you so . . . '

Bonnie held Maybelle as if she'd never let her go. She smelt her soap and lipstick. Smelt her skin. She *wouldn't* let her go. She shut her eyes tight, and everything was all right.'

Everything was *all right*.

'You wretched, WRETCHED, WRETCHED girl,' Maybelle said. 'I love you so. You've grown. You've changed. Just look at you now. Wherever have you been?' She looked up. Michael was standing in the doorway. 'You said she'd come back,' she said. 'You *said* she would.'

'I *promised* she would,' he said.

'You'd better come in too . . . '

They sat together on the settee in front of the little fireplace in what, once, might have been a sewing-room with a special painting on the wall. There was a small, bright rug on the bare floor. In the corner, in a pot, stood the huge plant with the floppy leaves. Maybelle had decorated it with silver Christmas balls. The fire crackled and blazed. There was a good pile of logs in a cardboard box, by its side. They sat together, Maybelle and Bonnie, with the dog watching Bonnie as Jake had done before he knew her and they became friends.

'He makes me feel safe, up here on my own,' Maybelle said. 'Do you like my sitting-room? There's still a lot to do, but it's the only room that's small enough to keep really warm. Do you like my velvet curtains? I bought them at the Christmas sale, down in the village. I've only just finished hanging them.'

Michael sat a little way apart. He leaned his head against the fire-breast wall. He smoked and watched them both. When Maybelle looked at him, he looked away and said nothing. Maybelle reached for a fresh log and threw it on the fire.

'I sawed this,' she said to him, proudly. '*You* said you didn't think I could do it. I saw logs every morning out on the terrace. And I mended the roof when the slates came off. And I don't mind being on my own. What do you think of that, then? I made a loaf today. Look . . . '

She reached among the remains of tea for a huge, heavy lump of bread, which she held aloft. Michael began to laugh at it, and she laughed as well. Michael shook his head and Maybelle flung herself back beside Bonnie. 'Oh, I'm so *happy* . . . '

You've changed as well, Bonnie thought. And it isn't awful like I thought it might be. It isn't like Doreen. You *can* run from hate. I didn't think you could once, but I know now. We've both done it.

'However did you find this place?' she said out loud. She pulled a bit off the end of the loaf, and ate it.

'I don't know.' Maybelle shook her head. 'It's got the same name as our block of flats. Funny, isn't it? I suppose that's what made me notice it. The farmer who owns it doesn't even make me pay rent. He says he's glad to have someone to keep it warm and keep the roof on. Can you imagine that? He lives in a bungalow down in the village. He doesn't even farm here any more. He thinks I'm crazy, staying up here. All the village does.

'I don't know how long I'll stay myself,' she went on. 'The novelty may wear off. I don't know where I'd be without my radio. We'll have to figure out how I'm going to get you down to school. It's such a long way down, and such a bumpy track.'

Michael threw his cigarette onto the fire. He got up. 'I'll leave you two,' he said. 'It's time for me to go.' He stretched himself.

'Go where?' Bonnie said, surprised, as Maybelle disappeared and returned with his coat and boots.

'Back down the hill, of course,' he said. 'Back to see if my poor old car will start. Back home.'

'But Michael . . . ' He was part of it all. He belonged up here. Didn't he know it? 'You can't go,' she said, feebly. 'It's too cold.'

'I've brought you home,' he said, struggling into his coat. 'It's what I promised, and I don't mind the cold. I like the snow. I'll enjoy walking in the dark and it's not too hard to keep to the track between the hedges.'

Maybelle handed him his boots, and he put them on.

'You've got to stay,' Bonnie said. 'I haven't told you yet about the land beyond.'

He smiled. 'There'll be another chance for that.' He dug into his pockets for his gloves. 'This time's just for you two,' he said.

Maybelle let him go. Bonnie followed him out into the hall, and then to the big front door which, judging from the struggle she had to open it, wasn't usually used here either.

'Thank you, Michael,' Bonnie heard her say and she couldn't believe it. Maybelle was showing him out. This was Michael, who'd made everything happen.

'You *can't* let him go, Maybelle,' she said, coming up beside her as Michael stamped along the terrace and down into the yard.

'He'll be back,' Maybelle said. 'Don't you know that?'

They stood and waved till he'd disappeared through the gate at the bottom. Then Maybelle shut the door and it was just the two of them, and Bonnie understood. She led Bonnie back towards the warm light of the sitting-room.

'We're on our own,' she said, happily. 'Like we always planned to be.' She stood in the half-open doorway with a backcloth of velvet curtains and flickering firelight on the wall. Bonnie remembered another night, somebody else's mother, questions she couldn't answer then.

'I think,' said Maybelle, and Bonnie knew it would be different now, 'the time has come for you to tell me where you've been.'

More stories from Lion Publishing

THE 'PANGUR BÁN' SERIES

Fay Sampson

Six beautiful, exciting adventures set in the
dramatic era of Celtic Britain.

SHAPE-SHIFTER: THE NAMING OF PANGUR BÁN
ISBN 0 7459 1347 4

PANGUR BÁN, THE WHITE CAT
ISBN 0 85648 580 2

FINNGLAS OF THE HORSES
ISBN 0 85648 899 2

FINNGLAS AND THE STONES OF CHOOSING
ISBN 0 7459 1124 2

THE SERPENT OF SERNARGAD
ISBN 0 7459 1520 5

THE WHITE HORSE IS RUNNING
ISBN 0 7459 1915 4

SHAPE-SHIFTER
The Naming of Pangur Bán

Fay Sampson

Deep in a dark cave in the Black Mountain, a witch was plotting mischief: 'We need something small, something sly, to carry a spell...and then we shall see who reigns on the Black Mountain!'

Shape-Shifter, the kitten, is her victim. But, before the charm is complete, he escapes. He finds himself caught in a spell that has gone wrong and a body that is not his own.

In blind panic, he brings disaster even to those who want to help him. Only a greater power can break the spell...

ISBN 0 7459 1347 4

PANGUR BÁN, THE WHITE CAT

Fay Sampson

The princess Finnglas is in the deadly grip of the
evil Sea Monster, deep down in the mysterious
underwater kingdom of the Sea Witch. And Niall
has been bewitched by the mermaids.

Pangur Bán, the white cat, is desperate. He must
rescue them—but how can he free them from
enchantment?

Only Arthmael can do it. But who is Arthmael?
Where is he? Can Pangur find him in time?

Shortlisted for the *Guardian* Children's Fiction
Award in 1984, this is the second book about
Finnglas and her friends.

ISBN 0 85648 580 2

THE 'AUSTIN FAMILY' SERIES

Madeleine L'Engle

Three classics of modern children's fiction. These vigorous, moving and often humorous books follow Vicky Austin through the highs and lows of early adolescence.

MEET THE AUSTINS
ISBN 0 7459 1385 7

THE MOON BY NIGHT
ISBN 0 7459 1384 9

A RING OF ENDLESS LIGHT
ISBN 0 7459 1383 0

MEET THE AUSTINS

Madeleine L'Engle

'It makes the grapefruit come out wrong, to have
five children, instead of four.'

It's not only the grapefruit which comes out
wrong when recently orphaned Maggy Hamilton
comes to stay. The Austin family are easy-going and
full of fun, but before long they all find their
patience and humour being put to the test. Seen
through the eyes of twelve-year-old Vicky, the
events following Maggy's arrival are often
surprising, sometimes sad, and occasionally
hilarious. But they're never dull.

This is the first book in the Austin Family series.

ISBN 0 7459 1385 7

More stories from Lion Publishing for you to enjoy